ERIC BLOODAXE

Ole Åsli
Tony Bakkejord

Envig AS

ENVIG
FORLAG

ISBN: 978-82-93794-80-6 (e-book)
ISBN: 978-82-93794-79-0 (paperback)
ISBN: 978-82-93794-78-3 (hardcover)

Cover design by: Ana Ristovska

Paperback and hardcover editions printed in the United States of America

CONTENTS

Southern Norway - 920 A.D.

Håløygaland

Selva

Lade

Trøndelag

Giske

Møre

Svanøy

Atløy

Firdafylke

Sogn

Hedmark

Hadeland

Hordaland

Romerike

Avaldsnes

Viken

Tønsberg

Rogaland

Agder

PART ONE

Gunnhild

CHAPTER: BJARMELAND

River Dvina, Bjarmeland, 922

'Down!'

Arinbjørn's heart pounded like a war drum as Eirik Haraldsson, his foster brother, charged at him with his bearded axe raised. Fear was a fleeting emotion, replaced by trust in Eirik's judgement. He dropped to his knees, and the axe swung over his head, close enough that he could hear the whistling of the blade, followed by a gruesome crunch of bone.

Turning, Arinbjørn saw a native with a split face slump to the ground. A rush of nausea swirled in his gut, but he swallowed it down, his training taking over.

'Pay attention to your surroundings,' Eirik warned as he pulled him back up, his blue eyes hardened with the ferocity of battle. His words held a note of concern, a reminder of their bond that transcended the battlefield.

'Thank you,' Arinbjørn replied, his voice shaky. The fear had dissipated, leaving in its wake a jarring awareness of his own mortality. 'I thought I was, but these fur people are everywhere.'

Eirik nodded, acknowledging his struggle. 'Yes, I did not expect them to be so many. Follow me!'

With renewed resolve, Arinbjørn gripped his axe firmly and followed Eirik, his breaths now matching the rhythm of his racing heart. The sense of urgency was palpable, their very survival hinged on their unity and quick actions.

As they approached the fur-clad natives, he noticed their eyes wide with fear, their bodies tensed for flight rather than fight. Eirik's frustrated roar of 'Stand your ground, you cowards!' echoed amid the chaos. He slowed down and caught a spear with his shield.

'It's like chasing seagulls,' Arinbjørn said. 'As soon as we get close, they take flight and land thirty paces further away.'

Turning back towards the settlement at the mouth of the river Dvina, the destruction became apparent. Huts burned, their flames reaching for the sky while figures darted in every direction amid the smoke. The cacophony of war cries mingled with the horrifying screams of fear and pain painted a grim picture.

'Pull back,' Eirik said, and grabbed Arinbjørn by the arm. 'They return in numbers. Pull back!'

'To the ships!' Eirik shouted as they ran back towards the river Dvina. 'Retreat!'

Looking over his shoulder, Arinbjørn saw a wave of fur-clad figures descend upon them. Panic flared, his breath hitching at the sight of scores of natives determined to repel the raiding Norwegians.

'There must be hundreds of them!'

'Torolv! Hauk!' Eirik shouted. 'Counterattack! Now!'

Arrows flew past them as they neared the village outskirts. To their left, a sudden shout marked a warrior's fall. Only moments later, an arrow found its mark in the back of another, sending him to the ground.

Arinbjørn skidded to a stop, dropping to a knee beside the fallen warrior. It was Hauk Håbrok, one of King Harald Fairhair's sturdiest soldiers. He called out, 'Hauk! Can you hear me?'

But Eirik cut him off, his voice sharp. 'No time for talking!

Help me lift him!'

Arinbjørn's shield hit the ground as he moved to help Eirik, grabbing Hauk under his right armpit. The wounded man grunted with pain.

'Torolv!' Eirik shouted.

Like a scene from a saga, Torolv Skallagrimsson burst on to the battlefield, backed by three dozen warriors. The natives reeled, their charge faltering in the face of the fresh Viking onslaught.

'Berg-Onund!' Eirik yelled above the fray. 'Help Arinbjørn get Hauk to the ships and yank that damned arrow out. Round up two dozen men and protect our looters.'

The moment Berg-Onund replaced him, Eirik charged ahead to stand with Torolv in the fray.

With considerable effort, Arinbjørn and Berg-Onund managed to lug Hauk back to the ships.

'Audun!' Arinbjørn called out as they approached. 'We need another set of hands.'

With the help of the seasoned warrior, they heaved Hauk on to one of the beached longships. Arinbjørn turned to Audun, worry furrowing his brow. 'Can you get the arrow out?'

Audun snorted. 'Any fool can pull out an arrow. You just have to pull hard enough.'

'I know that,' Arinbjørn replied, 'but—'

'You're asking about doing it right.' Audun cut him off, his eyes focused on Hauk's injury. 'Depends on the arrow and where it went in. First, we need his armour off. Hold him still.'

Without wasting a moment, Audun gripped the arrow's shaft and snapped it off. Hauk groaned in pain, a hopeful sign in the grim situation.

Once Hauk was stripped of his chain mail and undershirt, Audun examined the wound more closely. 'The arrowhead's not too deep,' he murmured, prodding the protruding shaft. He grimaced, pulling a knife from his belt. 'Stuck between the ribs, though. I'll have to wiggle it out.'

Offering Hauk his own belt, Audun said, 'Bite down on this.' When Hauk barely responded, Audun just shrugged and set to work. Moments later, he had the arrow free.

'A broadhead,' Audun mused, holding it up. 'Deadly for small game, not so much for armoured warriors.' He grinned at Hauk, who was drifting in and out of consciousness. 'Unless the wound festers, you'll live to fight another day.'

Arinbjørn let out a breath he hadn't realised he was holding. Standing, he surveyed the battlefield. There were no lines, no formations. The natives harassed the Norse with spears and arrows, steering clear of hand-to-hand combat unless they had the upper hand. There must have been at least three hundred of them—far more resistance than they'd seen elsewhere in Bjarmeland. Their usual tactic of a predawn raid was useless here in the land of the midnight sun. The villagers had plenty of time to spot their ships and prepare for the assault.

Drawing a deep breath, Arinbjørn scooped up a fresh shield. 'Tend to his wounds,' he told Audun. 'We'll have more wounded before the day's out.'

And with that, he sprang from the ship, racing back towards the fray.

CHAPTER: GUNNHILD

Finnmark, 922

Gunnhild rose and climbed out of the *goahti* to meet the approaching riders. The arctic wind whipped her face and tugged at her braided hair. She'd heard four horses but was not surprised when a fifth rider appeared over the hill, a few heartbeats after the others.

She stood still, revealing no emotion as the foreign warriors rode in circles around her and the primitive hut behind her. Southerners, surely. Taller than the local Sámi men and armed for battle. Or perhaps they've just seen battle, she mused, when she noticed the tears and imperfections in their armour and garments. Men were at their worst after a battle, whether they'd won or lost.

The most imposing of them reined in his horse in front of her. He wore chain mail, and a long sword hung from his belt. *A hersir or a hersir's son*, Gunnhild thought. Fair and handsome.

'I am Torolv, son of Skallagrim. Who are you, and where is your tribe?'

Gunnhild looked around and let her gaze rest on the goahti she'd lived in for almost six winters. When she looked back at the fair southerner, she stared him straight in the eyes.

'I am Gunnhild, daughter of Ossur Tote of Håløygaland. I have no tribe unless you count three as a tribe.'

Torolv dismounted and approached her, while his companions remained on their horses. He had that look, the one most men got in her company. The pitiful blend of desire and insecurity.

'What is the daughter of a wealthy man from southern Håløygaland doing among the Sámi in the far north? Are you someone's wife, or a captive?'

Gunnhild cocked her head and smirked.

'You know my father?'

'By name and reputation only. But you did not answer,' Torolv said.

'Well, Torolv Skallagrimsson, you shall have your answers. I'm neither a wife nor a captive. My father thought it wise that I'd spend some time with my mother's people in Finnmark to learn from the most powerful *noaidis* of all the Sámi.'

'What is a noaidi?'

Gunnhild shrugged. 'You would probably call them *seiðmenn*, or sorcerers.'

Torolv reached for his sword hilt. 'Accursed seiðmenn! Where are they?'

Gunnhild laughed. 'I did not say they were seiðmenn, as their powers are different from those of the seiðmenn in the south. But you have no word for what they are. The noaidis are out hunting, and two hundred of your kind wouldn't find them unless they wanted you to.'

'There are indeed two hundred of us, but most remain by the ships,' Torolv said.

'Is that so?' Gunnhild said. 'That would explain my violent dreams and the scent of blood and smoke. Was there a battle?'

'We return from a great victory in Bjarmeland,' Torolv said.

'Under which jarl?'

'Not a jarl. Eirik, son of King Harald Fairhair.'

Gunnhild shrugged. 'Then I suggest you return to the safety of your ships before my companions return. King Harald is not held in high regard in Finnmark.'

Torolv nodded. 'We shall leave, but you will come with us.'

'I wish I could, but the noaidis have powers beyond your imagination,' Gunnhild said, her voice dark and ominous. 'They are hunting now, but their lust for me is strong, and they will follow our trail like dogs through mud or snow. Nobody escapes them, and their arrows are true. If roused to anger, they can cause the earth to open and swallow you. Anything they look upon in wrath will fall dead to the ground.'

The four riders laughed, but Torolv silenced them with a stern glance.

'Now, you must leave before they return,' Gunnhild said.

'We shall not leave without you,' Torolv said.

Gunnhild sighed. Men were so predictable.

'Very well,' she said and nodded towards the primitive hut of stone, wood and peat. 'I will hide two of you here in the goahti, and you must try to not get yourself killed. The others must take the horses and flee. I will cover your tracks. Hurry, before they return.'

Torolv looked from man to man without saying anything. Eventually, he nodded and handed the reins to one of the others.

'Berg-Onund, you stay with me. Arinbjørn, take our horses and lead the others back to camp,' Torolv commanded.

'Wait!' Gunnhild said as the three riders prepared to leave with two spare horses in tow.

'What?' said Torolv.

'You will make too much noise with that armour, and you can't fight well with swords inside the hut. Keep your long knives and send the rest of your gear away with your friends.'

'Certainly not!' the man called Berg-Onund spat.

Torolv kept silent, thinking.

He can think as well, that one, Gunnhild mused.

'It's a trap, Torolv,' one of the riders said. He was short and young, no more than fifteen winters. 'You will be slain with only your seax to defend you.'

'My seax is sharp, Atle, and my chain mail will not defend me against a seiðmann's sorcery. Do as she says.'

'Join me inside when you're ready,' Gunnhild said. She knew what must be done. The noaidis, powerful as they were, stood between her and her escape. She had witnessed their powers, had seen them bend nature to their whims, and she knew that if she was to leave, they could not be allowed to live. Her heart pounded at the thought, the enormity of the task at hand seeping into her. But she steeled herself. Survival demanded sacrifices.

While Torolv and Berg-Onund doffed their armour, Gunnhild re-entered the goahti and scooped ashes into a leather bag. When the two southern warriors entered through the wooden door, she rose and handed them each two reindeer hides.

'You must hide,' Gunnhild implored. 'The noaidis are not men of steel and sword. They fight with forces that are not of this world, forces that your blade cannot hope to fend off. In their presence, you are helpless, and your strength is your curse. Lay against the walls on either side and cover your bodies with these. If any part of your bodies can be seen, you will be found and killed.'

'If their senses are as keen as you claim, won't they catch our scent or hear our breath?' Torolv asked.

'I will make sure their senses are busy,' Gunnhild said, and left the two warriors to find suitable hiding places.

Back outside, she chanted softly while strewing the ashes over the southerners' tracks. Before long, the leather bag was almost empty, and she spread the last handfuls over the goahti before she walked down to the stream to wash her hands and face. Once there, she decided she might as well cleanse her entire body in preparation for what was to come.

Gunnhild removed her necklaces and arm rings and pulled the serk over her head before she waded into the cold stream and crouched to wash herself. After the first few unpleasant moments, her skin numbed, and she could breathe normally again. She loosened her braids and plunged her head into the water to let the stream rinse her hair before getting back out.

She did not have to wait for long until the two noaidi returned. Only then did she pull the serk back over her head, allowing the men to catch a glimpse of her naked body from a distance. They almost stumbled over each other as they ran towards her.

'We saw tracks of men and horses. Have you spoken to anyone?' said Biejaš, in Sámi.

'Nobody has been here,' Gunnhild replied in imperfect Sámi. 'But I heard men and horses, so I covered our tracks and our home with ashes and hid inside. They came close, but they never found me.' She grinned proudly for added effect.

'You have done well,' said Ailo. 'We followed their tracks close to the goahti, but it seems they left without finding it.'

Gunnhild beamed.

They walked inside and rekindled the fire from the dying embers. Gunnhild was relieved to find that the two southern warriors had been thorough. If she had not known they were there, she would not have noticed any sign of them. Only the hides rolled up against the stone base of the walls revealed where they lay.

While Biejaš and Ailo prepared their meal, Gunnhild combed her hair, readied her bed, and endured their incessant hints and insinuations about sharing it with her. Their envy of the other offered all the protection she needed. Neither would suffer the pain of seeing the other man share Gunnhild's bed, and so they watched each other. Lately, the two noaidis had stayed awake until morning, fearing one might make his move if the other fell asleep. That would make her task easier this night.

After they'd shared their meal, Gunnhild went outside to wash her hands and face again. It was getting late, but it was still not dark so far north. There were more yellow than green leaves on the crooked mountain birches near the stream. Pink heather covered the ground. It was quite beautiful here, but this might be her last night in the far north.

'Now,' Gunnhild said, once she was back inside, 'come here and lie down, one on each side of me.'

Biejaš and Ailo eagerly accepted her invitation. Gunnhild laid an arm round the neck of each and chanted softly. Soon, the two sleep-deprived noaidis fell asleep. She shook Ailo, enough to wake him up, but he fell back to sleep again instantly. Biejaš hardly stirred, even when she squeezed his shoulder.

Gunnhild reached for two seal-skin bags, pulled them over the heads of the two noaidis, and tied them fast under their arms.

'Come now, Torolv,' she whispered.

Torolv and Berg-Onund rolled out from under the reindeer hides with long knives in hand. Moments later, they'd executed the two helpless noaidis and dragged them out of the hut.

'Are you ready to come with us?' Torolv asked Gunnhild when he returned with Berg-Onund. 'If we go now, we might get there before it gets too dark to see.'

'Not tonight,' Gunnhild said in a grave tone. 'The spirits will be angry and eager to punish us for what we did. We stand a better chance if we spend the night here.'

Even as she spoke, the shadows grew darker and threatened to swallow the light from the fireplace.

They spent a restless night in the goahti, between a trembling ground and a thundering sky.

CHAPTER: EIRIK HARALDSSON

Finnmark

The camp fell into an eerie silence as Torolv, Berg-Onund and Gunnhild made their way towards the shore. Whispers hushed and countless eyes turned to gaze upon them, particularly Gunnhild. She was no stranger to such reactions from men and took pleasure in returning their glances, causing them to avert their eyes.

Berg-Onund eventually located his brother, Atle, while Torolv guided Gunnhild towards a magnificent ship. It may not have been the largest vessel, with only twelve oars, but its beauty was undeniable. The sail boasted vibrant hues of green and blue, while the hull was adorned with an array of bright colours. Torolv paused a few paces away from a tall, black-haired man inspecting an area where the paint had scraped off.

'My Lord Eirik,' Torolv said, 'we have discovered a hersir's daughter sharing a hut with two Sámi seiðmenn.'

'Welcome back, Torolv,' Eirik replied, his voice devoid of emotion as he continued his examination without facing them. 'Bind her with the other thralls. Her ransom should fetch a decent price.'

'Perhaps you should lay eyes on her first,' Torolv suggested.

Eirik finally turned his attention towards Gunnhild, and their gazes locked. Unlike most men, he did not shy away from her stare. Instead, his eyes narrowed slightly, and a faint twitch played at the corners of his mouth.

'I am Eirik Haraldsson, son of King Harald Fairhair. And who might you be?'

The king's son possessed an aura of strength and vitality, despite not being conventionally handsome.

'I am Gunnhild. My father is Ossur Tote of Håløygaland, a merchant and hersir under the jarl of Lade. I have been residing with my mother's kin in Finnmark,' Gunnhild responded.

Eirik glanced at Torolv, who quickly averted his gaze.

'A worthy ransom indeed,' Eirik smirked. 'She may be small, but undoubtedly a grown woman, and pleasing to the eye. If her father refuses to pay, I'm certain others will. Find some food for both of you and bring her aboard my ship. I suspect I will find her company quite enjoyable.'

'Very well,' Torolv acknowledged, taking hold of Gunnhild's arm to lead her away.

Gunnhild had to quicken her steps to match Torolv's stride as they made their way back to the camp. Soon, they each received a bowl of rye gruel and a few pieces of stockfish.

'How do you know my father?' Gunnhild inquired, her fingers working meticulously over a small piece of dried fish.

'I don't,' Torolv responded. His voice was weighted with a gruffness that seemed to come from the encounter with Eirik Haraldsson.

'You said his name as if it holds a meaning for you. You claimed knowledge of him,' Gunnhild said, her tone gently pressing.

'Yes, I have knowledge of him, it's true,' Torolv admitted after a moment's pause. 'I may not have grown up in Håløygaland, but my lineage has long held an understanding of the prominent families who preside over those lands. My grandfather was a hersir of his own right, ruling over the lands of Firdafylke. But he left our homeland for the distant shores of Iceland, running from the wrath of Harald Fairhair.'

Gunnhild, still nursing her dried fish, shot a quick, piercing glance at him. 'And yet, it appears that you now journey under the banner of Fairhair's son?'

'Harald Fairhair himself would not open his halls to me, seeing my kinship with those he saw as enemies. But his son Eirik saw something of worth in me, and he has welcomed me into his own fold,' Torolv explained, his gaze steady and unflinching, despite the probing nature of Gunnhild's questions.

'And what convinced Eirik Haraldsson, son of a king, to extend his friendship to an outsider, the grandson of an exiled hersir?' Gunnhild probed further, her curiosity as sharp as a honed blade.

'Well, as it happens,' Torolv said, a small, self-satisfied smile tugging at the corners of his mouth, 'I found favour in Eirik's eyes through the very means we Vikings appreciate most —the gift of a fine ship, sturdy and swift. The very same ship you saw docked on your shore today.'

CHAPTER: VOYAGE

As the ship sailed south with the shores of Finnmark on its port side, Gunnhild stood near the prow and observed Eirik overseeing the navigation of the ship. There was an air of command and confidence in his movements, coupled with a hint of vulnerability that intrigued her. She made her way towards him, her steps steady despite the rhythmic sway of the vessel.

Eirik glanced in her direction. 'Enjoying the journey, Gunnhild?' he asked, a faint smile gracing his lips.

Gunnhild nodded, but before she found the words to reply, Eirik spoke again, his eyes sparkling with appreciation. 'There is something liberating about sailing these waters, far away from the constraints of land. Tell me, Gunnhild, what drew you to Finnmark and the Sámi people?'

Gunnhild leaned against the ship's railing, her gaze fixed on the horizon. 'My father believed it was important for me to connect with my mother's kin, to learn from the powerful noaidis of the Sámi. It was an opportunity to understand the ancient ways and harness the wisdom that resides within their traditions.'

'And what have you learnt during your time among the Sámi people? What wisdom do you carry with you?'

Gunnhild turned her attention back to Eirik, her eyes gleaming with a depth of knowledge. 'I have come to understand the delicate balance of nature, how all living beings are connected. The Sámi have taught me to respect the land and its spirits, to listen to the whispers of the wind and the secrets of the rivers. They possess a deep connection to the unseen realms.'

Eirik's brow furrowed slightly, contemplation etched across his features. 'I have heard tales of the Sámi's abilities, their sorcery and seiðmann practices. Are you skilled in their arts, Gunnhild?'

Gunnhild's lips curled into a knowing smile. 'I have acquired some understanding of their ways, Eirik. The noaidis have shared fragments of their wisdom with me, allowing me glimpses into realms beyond our comprehension. It is a path I tread cautiously, for such power comes with great responsibility.'

Eirik's gaze locked on to Gunnhild's. 'You are an unusual woman, Gunnhild. There is a strength and resilience in you that sets you apart.'

Gunnhild's smile widened, a hint of mischief in her eyes. 'And what about you, Eirik? What lies beneath your stern demeanour? There is a fire within you, a burning ambition to forge your own fate. Tell me, what drives you to these shores?'

Eirik's expression softened, a flicker of vulnerability surfacing. 'I know I must prove myself, to step out from my father's shadow. I yearn to carve my own path, though I don't yet know how or where it will take me.'

'Perhaps our paths have converged for a reason,' Gunnhild said.

Eirik's gaze lingered on Gunnhild's face. 'Perhaps.'

CHAPTER: OSSUR TOTE

Håløygaland

'Welcome home, Gunnhild!' The familiar voices of her brothers filled the air as Gunnhild stepped on to the pier. Alv and Øyvind stood there, grown and changed since she had last seen them.

'You've grown so much,' Gunnhild remarked, a smile playing on her lips. 'How old are you now? Thirty and twenty-eight?'

The brothers burst into laughter, shaking their heads. 'No, not even close! I've seen thirteen winters, and Øyvind eleven,' Alv replied, his eyes sparkling with amusement.

Chuckling, Gunnhild conceded, 'Well, the winters in Finnmark are longer, you know. That's why I'm so wise for my age.'

Øyvind, always eager to find a point of pride, chimed in, 'But I'm taller than you!'

Gunnhild, unfazed by her brother's height, replied with a mischievous grin, 'I'm not limited by my stature, Øyvind. I can be as large or small as I choose to be.' She deepened her voice, adopting an eerie tone that made her brothers' eyes widen.

'You're a shape-changer?' Øyvind asked, his curiosity piqued.

Leaning closer, Gunnhild whispered, 'Shh ... don't speak of

such things. It's our little secret.'

Both boys nodded eagerly, their imaginations ignited by the possibility of their sister's hidden powers.

'Good. Let's go see our dear father,' Gunnhild said, placing a hand on each brother's shoulder. Together, they made their way towards the longhouse, walking amid the warm greetings and kind words of the residents. Gunnhild could not help but notice the changes that had taken place during her absence. The new brewhouse and the increased number of servants and thralls were evidence of her father's prosperity. It brought her some solace, knowing that he might be better equipped to handle the demands that lay ahead.

Their reunion was interrupted by the arrival of Torolv, Eirik and the young Arinbjørn, who caught up with them. Gunnhild's heart sank at the realisation that they were about to face her father, who would not be amenable if he found Eirik's demands unreasonable.

'I think it best we meet your father together and make the necessary arrangements,' Eirik said.

A house thrall held the door open for them to enter the longhouse. There were three new tapestries along the wall, another indication her father had prospered in Gunnhild's absence. At the high seat, Ossut seemed unprepared and uncomfortable with the unexpected visit, barely sparing a glance at his daughter. After a few heartbeats of awkward silence, Torolv stepped forward and spoke.

'Our honourable host, Ossut. I am Torolv, son of Skallagrim, son of Kveldulv. Let me introduce Eirik Haraldsson, King Harald Fairhair's son, and heir to the throne of Norway. In our company is also Arinbjørn, son of Tore Roaldsson of Svanøy. And this young woman, Gunnhild, rescued from captivity in Finnmark. She claims to be your daughter. Does she speak the truth?'

Ossut hesitated before rising from his seat, fixing his gaze on Gunnhild. He approached her, studying her face with a mix of recognition and contemplation. Finally, a smile crossed his lips, and he embraced her.

'Are you well?' Ossut whispered, his voice filled with concern.

'I am,' Gunnhild replied.

'I'm sorry about your mother. I would have sent for you if I'd known she passed away when you were still so young,' he said.

'She did not survive the first winter. But our kin accepted me as one of their own, and I have lacked for nothing,' Gunnhild said.

Ossut pulled away from the embrace, resuming his role as the host.

'This is Gunnhild, my daughter. I thank you for returning her to me,' Ossut announced, acknowledging the efforts of Eirik and his men.

Eirik seized the moment. 'My men risked their own lives to rescue her from captivity with two Sámi sorcerers. I believe we're entitled to a ransom.'

Ossut looked to Gunnhild, who looked down and shook her head slightly.

'I see ...,' Ossut said and returned to his seat. He waved at a middle-aged servant and whispered something to him. When the servant disappeared, Ossut spoke.

'As much as I'm surprised by your visit, Eirik Haraldsson, I'm even more surprised to find Torolv Skallagrimsson in your company. Your father's betrayal and murder of his uncle, Torolv Kveldulvsson, is known to every man and woman in Håløygaland.'

Gunnhild gasped, and Eirik's expression soured. But it was Torolv who spoke first.

'The story is, of course, well known to us all, Ossut. But

we've found it unfair to judge an innocent man for his father's crimes.'

'You have a generous heart, Torolv Skallagrimsson. Might I also assume that Harald Fairhair has forgiven your father for murdering his uncle Guttorm's sons before he fled to Iceland?' Ossut said.

'I would advise against making assumptions on your king's behalf,' Eirik said.

Ossut shrugged and turned to the servant, who had returned to his side with a leather pouch. Ossut weighed it in his hands, returned it, and nodded. The balding servant kept his head low as he approached Eirik and handed him the pouch.

'Half a mark—a generous ransom for my daughter,' said Ossut.

Eirik smiled as he tossed the pouch in the air and caught it. 'You prove your honour and loyalty to your family when you put such a high price on your daughter's life. Therefore, I'm sure you will be delighted to know that I offer to double your price.'

What's this? Gunnhild thought.

Ossut frowned. 'What do you mean? Do you demand a full mark as a ransom for my daughter? Truly, that would be extortion, a price beyond what can be expected from any man.'

'Truly,' said Eirik. 'That's why I offer a full mark of gold for your daughter's hand in marriage.'

Gunnhild looked down at the floor and swallowed. Eirik had two dozen warriors at his immediate disposal, and another two ships lay in wait. If her father failed to recognise the peril of opposing such a force, her family and home might be destroyed.

Eirik held up the leather pouch Ossut had given him. 'And this half mark I give to Gunnhild to use as she pleases.'

When Ossut remained silent, Eirik continued, 'If my honourable host would like to spend a few days and nights contemplating my proposal, I'm happy to oblige. I only ask that my men are provided with sleeping quarters, food and drink.'

Gunnhild's gaze fell to the floor, her stomach knotting with unease. The weight of Eirik's forces hung heavily in the air, their presence a palpable threat to her family and home. *That's a threat, Father,* she thought. *Eirik's army will devour your stores of meat and drink before the long winter.*

Ossut, his resolve tested, rose and slowly approached Eirik, extending his arm in acceptance.

'Very well, Eirik Haraldsson. I accept your proposal and invite you and your hird to feast with us tonight to celebrate your betrothal!'

Eirik's smile widened as he firmly shook Ossut's hand, sealing their agreement.

With that, Gunnhild's fate was irrevocably sealed, and the weight of uncertainty settled upon her.

CHAPTER: TOROLV KVELDULVSSON

Håløygaland

'Marriage?! Could you not just collect your ransom and leave me with my father?'

Gunnhild didn't shout, but her voice was loud enough for everyone on board to hear. She had refrained from arguing with Eirik during the feast the night before, but as soon as they were on the ship, she could not hold back. The crew did their best to look busy handling their tasks as they set sail for their journey south.

'No. I've come to enjoy your company,' Eirik responded, the corners of his mouth turning up into a smirk. His eyes, however, didn't mirror the same mirth.

'I haven't seen you enjoy anything since the day we met!' Gunnhild countered, her voice echoing against the hull of the ship.

'I've been bored. I'm looking to remedy that.'

Gunnhild's hand tightened around the wooden rail, her knuckles whitening. 'I'm not your cure for boredom!'

The corners of Eirik's lips twisted into a ghost of a smile again. This time, a spark of amusement flickered in his eyes. 'Would you rather stay behind in your hut and marry one of the seiðmenn?'

Gunnhild's cheeks flushed crimson. 'I'd rather marry

Torolv. At least he's kind and handsome.'

Eirik chuckled at her response, shaking his head lightly as he looked out over the rippling water. 'Torolv is also wise enough to know that he would not live to see another sunset if he stole my bride. Besides, I believe he has someone else in his sights.'

Gunnhild was silent for a moment, her thoughts a whirlwind. She blinked, and when she spoke again, her voice was steely. 'I'm not yours to claim, you arrogant brute!'

Eirik turned to face her, his smile fading. His eyes softened, taking on an unexpected warmth as he looked at her. 'Your father willingly consented to our union. But you're right, I am a brute. And probably arrogant, though I'm not quite sure what you mean by that.'

Eirik's smile stirred something within Gunnhild, something she found hard to pinpoint. She found herself at a loss for words.

'When I was just a boy of twelve, my father gifted me three longships,' Eirik continued. 'After that, I spent four years living the life of a Viking in the west, and then another four leading raids in the east. Last winter, I resided with my foster father on Svanøy, but when spring came, I ventured north to Bjarmeland. I fought hard and won great victories there. I was on my journey back when I crossed paths with you. So, you are not wrong: I'm more a warrior than a smooth talker, especially when it comes to beautiful women. Stay with me and help me embrace a life that's not all about fighting,' Eirik said.

Gunnhild paused, considering the man before her and wondering if there was more to him than met the eye.

'Your father and I made another agreement last night,' Eirik continued.

'Of course you did,' Gunnhild responded, her tone laced with scepticism. 'What now? Did you persuade him to serve you? Did you purchase his farm with a few more pieces of gold?'

'No, nothing like that,' Eirik reassured her. 'We agreed that your brothers will travel south next summer. They will train with my guards. Depending on their growth and how quickly they learn, they may spend the winter on Svanøy or at my father's estate in Avaldsnes.'

Gunnhild felt her anger towards Eirik ebbing away, leaving her feeling somewhat deflated.

'Well, thank you. That's thoughtful of you,' she managed.

'My pleasure,' Eirik said. 'A queen needs strong warriors she can trust.'

Gunnhild was quiet for a moment, her gaze fixed on the waves as she tried to assemble her thoughts. Finally, she breathed in and spoke.

'Eirik Haraldsson, you're a man of many facets. Allow me time to understand you, and maybe we can make this marriage work.'

Eirik smiled. 'Absolutely.'

'Thank you,' Gunnhild said, then she walked away. She watched the crew busy with their tasks and had a short chat with Berg-Onund and Arinbjørn, two of the young raiders from Torolv's crew. Afterwards, she found Torolv and observed him as he busied himself with ropes and knots.

'Is it true?' Gunnhild said.

'What?' Torolv replied, glancing back at her.

'About King Fairhair killing your uncle, like my father said.'

'That's what they say.'

'Was your uncle against the king?'

'Not at all. He was a faithful member of the king's guard.'

'So, how did it happen?'

Torolv finished securing a rope, then turned back to her.

'I only know what my father told me. I wasn't born yet when my uncle died.'

Torolv gestured towards an empty sailor's chest nearby, inviting Gunnhild to take a seat before joining her.

'It's quite a tale.'

'We have all the time in the world,' Gunnhild grinned. 'Just skip the dull parts.'

Torolv, lost in thought, nodded.

'About fifty years ago, my Uncle Torolv was part of King Harald's guard. During the decisive battle at Hafrsfjord, he was seriously injured while defending the king's ship. He survived though.'

'I guessed that.'

'Bård Brynjolfsson from Håløygaland, another one of the king's guards, was also injured. While Torolv got better, Bård didn't. Knowing he was dying, Bård asked to talk to King Harald Fairhair. Harald came and listened to Bård's last words.'

Torolv paused, clearing his throat before continuing in a deep voice.

'If I die from these injuries, I want to pick who gets my inheritance. I want Torolv, my friend, to have my land, my estates and my wife. I also want him to raise my son because I trust Torolv more than anyone else.'

'That's a big responsibility, but I guess your uncle was up for it if he was anything like you.'

Torolv seemed to ignore the comment.

'The king agreed right away, as was the custom. The next day, Bård died. Once Torolv was better, King Harald dismissed him from service. Later that year, my uncle travelled north to Håløygaland with sixty soldiers. He moved on to Bård's farm in Torgar and married Bård's widow, Sigrid.'

'And Sigrid agreed to this? It was her land, and she might have wanted to marry someone else.'

'She could have lost everything, which is why Bård chose Torolv.'

'Why so?'

'Years ago, when Bård's grandfather—Bjørgolv—was old, he went to a feast at Hogne's house, a rich farmer in Leka. There, the host's beautiful daughter, Hilderid, caught his eye. That same year, Bjørgolv returned with thirty men and demanded to marry Hilderid. Hogne had no choice but to accept and took one ounce of gold as payment for his daughter.'

Gunnhild doubled over, feeling a sudden pain in her stomach.

'What's wrong? Are you sick?' Torolv asked.

'No,' Gunnhild said, looking down at her feet. 'I just realised that I was bought in the same way.'

Torolv paused and gently touched her shoulder. 'I'm sorry. I didn't think about that.'

Gunnhild nodded, taking deep breaths to steady herself.

'At least Eirik paid eight times more for you,' Torolv added.

Gunnhild cringed at the thought, but then she laughed. 'I suppose that gives me bragging rights! Thanks for that!' She rested her head against Torolv's shoulder. 'Okay, I can handle this. Please keep going.'

'Are you sure?'

'Yes, I can't wait to hear about poor Hilderid.'

'Well, Bjørgolv and Hilderid moved to Torgar and had two sons, Hårek and Rørek. When Bjørgolv died, Brynjolf sent Hilderid and her boys back to Leka.'

'That was harsh,' Gunnhild commented.

'Maybe,' Torolv replied, 'but I don't feel bad for Hilderid or her boys. Soon after my uncle settled in Torgar, Hårek and Rørek claimed their father's farm and lands. Torolv denied them because their mother was taken by force, and children from such unions have no inheritance rights.'

Gunnhild nodded, and Torolv continued.

'The Hilderidssons knew they could not beat Torolv. He was a friend of the king and a famous warrior with lots of soldiers. Over the years, Torolv's wealth grew. He got more land and sailed to Finnmark to trade and collect tributes. And he was always loyal to King Fairhair and paid his taxes.'

'Sounds like a good man,' Gunnhild observed.

'He was, from what I've heard. But the Hilderidssons tricked Harald Fairhair into thinking that Torolv was keeping the king's taxes for himself and gaining power to oppose him. So, Fairhair sailed north with a strong army and set fire to Torolv's house. There was a big fight. At first, the burning house protected Torolv and his men. But soon, the fire was so intense that they had to abandon their defence positions. Torolv charged at King Harald, but he was stopped just three feet away from him. Harald killed Torolv and ordered the battle to stop.'

'I'm sorry to hear that. Did your father escape to Iceland after this?'

'Not right away. My father, Skallagrim, confronted King Harald and demanded compensation for his brother's death. Harald consented, but only if Skallagrim served him like Torolv did. My father declined, saying if Torolv's service wasn't good enough, his wouldn't be either. This made the king angry, and my father had to run away to avoid being killed.'

'Harald Fairhair sounds cruel.'

'He can be, depending on who you are. The king is kind to his friends and harsh to his enemies. My family has seen both sides.'

'Fair enough. But I don't understand why the king has held a grudge against your family for so long. After all, he started the fight.'

'True, but there's more to the story.'

'Tell me!'

'My father and my grandfather, Kveldulv, escaped on a

ship. But along the way, they encountered another ship that had belonged to Torolv before the king took it. With forty men, they attacked and didn't stop until everyone on the other ship was dead or had jumped overboard.'

'Your family can be quite ruthless too.'

'Indeed. Two of the boys who drowned were the sons of Guttorm Sigurdsson, Harald's uncle and trusted advisor. The boys were on their way to live with Harald because Guttorm had died.'

'Oh, no!'

'Harald loved Guttorm, and I doubt he'll ever forgive my family for killing his kin. Kveldulv was injured in the fight and knew he wouldn't make it to Iceland. He asked his crew to build a coffin and throw him overboard when he died, and that my father should build a new home where he washed ashore. My father found Kveldulv's coffin on the northern shore of a fjord on the western coast, and that's where he built Borg. We've lived there ever since.'

'But how did you become friends with Harald's son? Didn't he know about his father's conflict with your family?'

'He knew. But when I came to Svanøy on this ship that I'd captured during a raid, I found Eirik admiring it. I decided to give it to him, and we've been friends since, despite Harald making it clear that he'll never meet me.'

Torolv glanced at Gunnhild and smiled. 'Turns out Eirik is enthralled by beauty.'

CHAPTER: STAD

Stad, Sogn

Three days out from Håløygaland, Gunnhild stood firm at the aft, her eyes narrowing as she surveyed the uneasy seas that lay ahead. Overhead, clouds began to merge into an ominous grey mass, casting a shadow as foreboding as the notorious Stad looming on the horizon. As anticipation mounted, the usual banter among the crew died down to whispered acknowledgements of the upcoming trial.

Eirik's gaze was hard and unyielding as he surveyed the gathering storm. His voice cut through the growing tension like a blade.

'Prepare yourselves! The sea intends to challenge us!'

Young Arinbjørn, whose spirit was typically as buoyant as their vessel, now mirrored Eirik's focus, the severity of the situation reflected in his grim expression.

Gunnhild touched the amulet of Freya that hung around her neck. It had been her mother's, and always brought her a sense of peace and protection. But now, faced with nature's fury and the lives of men at stake, it felt like a small and powerless thing.

As the storm descended, waves battered the ship and the wind shrieked through the rigging, transforming their peaceful voyage into a battle against the sea's fury. Gunnhild clenched the ropes, her knuckles turning white. She watched the crew rise to the challenge, their movements swift. Eirik, at the steering oar, seemed to meet each wave as though it were a personal challenge.

'Hard to port! Keep her steady,' Eirik's command echoed, his eyes tracking the waves.

'Secure those ropes! Stay vigilant!' Arinbjørn's voice followed, bolstering Eirik's orders.

Gunnhild watched as Torolv, known for his hearty voice, silently moved through the crew. His actions were precise and efficient—securing ropes, stabilising cargo and offering support as he went. His serene demeanour sparked a quiet admiration within her. This peaceful observation was abruptly shattered by a massive wave that crashed on to the deck, soaking her and the rest of the crew.

A desperate cry cut through the storm's din as the next giant wave swept Berg-Onund overboard. Gunnhild's heart pounded in her chest as she watched Eirik, without a moment's hesitation, hand the steering oar to Arinbjørn and dive into the frothing sea, a rope clutched tightly in his grasp.

As Eirik made his plunge, Torolv quickly seized command. His voice, strong and clear, rang out over the storm. 'Hold steady, Arinbjørn! Tighten those ropes, Atle!' He moved with purpose, his actions providing a steadying presence.

Despite the looming peril, Gunnhild could not suppress the urge to peer over the port rim. Wave after wave crashed over her back, each an icy reminder of the dangers below. But her gaze remained on the tumultuous sea, searching for any sign of Eirik. With each passing wave, Eirik's rope unspooled further, until only the end, firmly tied to the ship, remained.

Gunnhild clutched her amulet of Freya and mouthed a silent plea before she cast it into the spitting sea. Time seemed to freeze as her senses sharpened, amplifying the roar of the waves and the howls of the wind. Then, she saw a dark shadow surfacing behind a towering wave before plunging back into the churning depths. Eirik.

With every muscle in her body tensed, Gunnhild wrapped

her fingers around the wet, twisted rope. She felt a vibration along the line, then a series of pulls. Two short, one long.

"Prepare to haul!" Torolv bellowed.

As the crew positioned themselves along the length of the rope, Gunnhild backed off and left the heavy work to the men. With a collective roar, they hauled, again and again. She turned back to the sea, waiting for Eirik to appear between the waves.

"Steady! Hold!" Torolv commanded behind her.

Gunnhild turned and saw the rope hanging limp in their hands. 'What is happening?'

Torolv looked up at her, grimacing. 'We lost him. Or he lost the rope.'

'Give them slack, now!' Arinbjørn's voice cracked through the air. 'Prepare to haul them in the moment you feel a tug!'

Gunnhild reached for the rope, her heart pounding with an urgency. A conflict erupted within her. She knew that jumping in would be futile. If Eirik succumbed to the raging sea, what chance did she stand? Why would she even consider sacrificing herself for a man who had purchased her against her will?

'Over there!' Atle called, pulling her back from her brief spell of contemplation.

Gunnhild turned even further behind, to look in the direction Atle was pointing, but saw nothing but the angry sea.

But then, twenty paces away, Eirik resurfaced with Berg-Onund clutched tightly to his side and the rope wrapped around one hand. The crew sprang back into action, pulling the rope and dragging their comrades back on board. A chorus of cheers erupted, momentarily drowning out the howling wind.

With a surge of water and foam, Eirik emerged from the ocean, one arm wrapped around Berg-Onund, the other clutching the rescue rope. Both men were hauled back onto the ship, their expressions a mix of exhaustion and unspoken gratitude. Eirik's eyes met Gunnhild's for a fleeting moment before he stumbled aft to Arinbjørn and took over the steering oar.

'I'll take over here,' Eirik said. 'Look to Berg-Onund.'

Moments later, Berg-Onund, too, was back on his feet.

As the ship finally passed the treacherous waters of the Stad, the sea's wrath seemed to quiet, as if appeased by their resilience. The tension among the crew abated as they returned to their routines.

Gunnhild exhaled deeply, her eyes meeting Eirik's. In that gaze, she found a complex tangle of relief, respect, and unspoken questions that would have to wait for another day. She allowed her eyes to close as she leaned back against the boards, welcoming the calm after the storm. Her fingers traced the empty space around her neck where her amulet used to be. She wondered if the sea had accepted her offering or if it was a prelude to challenges yet to come. Either way, she sensed that the voyage was far from over.

They had weathered their first storm.

CHAPTER: SVANØY

Svanøy, Firdafylke

As they approached the island of Svanøy, Gunnhild found herself captivated by the blossoming scenery. The eastern expanse of the island was flat, the monotony broken by the forested hills rising in the west. Ahead, farmhouses huddled in clusters, and a pier stretched out alongside a small gathering of buildings.

'Welcome to Svanøy,' Eirik said, wrapping his arms around Gunnhild. 'This is the land where I was raised under the guidance of Tore Roaldsson, Arinbjørn's father.'

They revelled in the scenery until the crew had fastened the vessel to the pier. Eirik's joy was contagious as he helped Gunnhild off the ship and guided her through his childhood haven, sharing tales of his youthful adventures. This was, undeniably, his home.

As they approached the main longhouse, Torolv Skallagrimsson was waiting caught up with them.

'My lord,' said Torolv, his eyes uncharacteristically downcast, 'may I have a word?'

Eirik frowned, his customary look of concern. 'Of course, Torolv.' He let go of Gunnhild and nodded for her to leave.

'Gunnhild can stay,' Torolv said.

Gunnhild looked to Eirik for confirmation. After a brief pause, Eirik nodded again. Slowly, this time. Both of them turned to Torolv.

'My lord, I beseech your leave to return to Iceland and visit my ailing parents. Your service has seen me travel far and wide, amassing a wealth of riches. However, my parents are now in their twilight years, and I yearn to share their company before their time arrives.'

Eirik's grimace suggested he was lost in thought. Finally, he responded, 'You've been more than a friend since our first meeting. As a leader of men and my trusted advisor, your absence will be deeply felt. While I understand your reasons, it pains me to let you go.'

'You honour me, my lord,' Torolv replied. 'I will always be your friend, but from now on you will spend much of your time with Gunnhild. I trust she will be as loyal a friend and adviser as I have been. As for leading your men in battle, your foster brother, Arinbjørn, has all the markings of a commander. He is loyal and as clever as any man, and he keeps calm in battle and rough weather. With some experience, he will surpass me in most regards.'

Eirik bit his lip, a blush creeping across his cheeks. 'No,' he voiced resolutely, 'I won't allow this.'

There was a plea in Torolv's eyes. A weighty silence fell between the two men, neither finding the words to bridge the gap. Sensing the tension, Gunnhild knew she had to intervene.

'Consider this more thoughtfully, Eirik,' she gently advised. 'You shouldn't let your heart alone dictate your decisions. I understand your bond with Torolv is strong, and the prospect of his departure is painful. Yet, with time, perspectives can change.'

With a bittersweet smile in Torolv's direction, Gunnhild softly took Eirik by the arm and guided him away. In silence, they walked arm in arm to the entrance of the grand longhouse.

Inside the longhouse, lit by flickering torches, a spectacle of shields, carvings, and vibrant tapestries welcomed them. A pleasant aroma of unfamiliar flowers and herbs filled the air as servants hurriedly prepared the feast. At the long table, Arinbjørn was deep in conversation with an older man who rose as the guests entered the hall.

'Ah, there you are!' the man said as he came to greet them. He must have seen fifty winters or more, but he was still appealing to the eye. His back was straight and his hair—more grey than black—was clean and combed back. There was a hint of grey on his chin and cheeks, indicating that he had shaved the day before. The eyes were narrow and sharp. A charming and wise man, Gunnhild surmised.

He grabbed Eirik's forearm and clasped his shoulder.

'Good to see you, Eirik! Arinbjørn told me you had to work harder for your plunder this time?'

Eirik's sour expression melted, and he managed to smile.

'Good to see you, too, Tore. I've missed Svanøy. And you, of course,' he added, just a little too late.

Tore burst out laughing. 'Ah, shut your mouth, boy! Of course you haven't missed the old man on your adventures. Especially not with this beauty by your side. Perhaps you could introduce us?'

Eirik cleared his throat. 'Yes, of course. Gunnhild, this is Tore Roaldsson. Arinbjørn's father and my foster father. He is the king's trusted man in this region. And this is Gunnhild, my betrothed. Daughter of Ossur Tote of Håløygaland.'

Tore smiled warmly at her. 'Truly enchanting!' he offered. 'You will have to win many battles to make yourself deserving of this one.'

Gunnhild beamed and retorted, 'Eirik, or I?'

'Both, I believe,' Tore replied with a wink. 'But please, join us for a meal and some rest after your voyage. The venison is particularly savoury.'

CHAPTER: TORA

Tore's meal was a lavish feast, a decadent array of mead, beer, and exotic Frankish wine. The succulent deer, as flavourful as the host had promised, vied for attention with hearty portions of pork and mutton, and rich, oily herring and mackerel. Accompanying these were loaves of fresh-baked barley and wheat bread, copious slabs of cheese, and generous dollops of butter. As the guests' appetite waned, the diligent servants whisked away their plates, only to replace them with sweet honey cakes, crisp apples, and juicy plums.

Over the course of the feast, as the discussions around the table diverged to various topics, Eirik found himself engrossed in talks of new trading prospects with Tore and Arinbjørn. Seeing this, Gunnhild seized the opportunity to engage in a private conversation with Torolv.

'This was where you met Eirik when he was twelve?'

'Yes,' Torolv mumbled, his words slightly garbled by a mouthful of juicy plum. 'My ship is moored in the very same spot as then.'

'How did you dare to return to Norway, to Harald's trusted hersir? Surely, you must have known the king would not welcome you with open arms?'

'I knew, and he didn't,' Torolv replied. 'But Tore Roaldsson was a fosterling at my grandfather Kveldulv's farm, and he's always been a friend of my father.'

'I didn't know that,' Gunnhild said. 'There are so many ties and connections between the prominent families.'

'That is true. But there was another reason I dared return to Norway when I did.'

'Really? What?'

'I was pleading for another man's life.'

'Do tell!'

'In Sogn, a full day's voyage south of here, there lived a wealthy and doughty young man called Bjørn Brynjolfsson.'

'Another Brynjolfsson! Bård's brother?' Gunnhild suggested.

'No, a different Brynjolf. There is no relation between the two.'

'Oh,' said Gunnhild. 'Please go on.'

'Well, Bård met a fair maiden at a feast and fell in love with her. She was Tora Lacehand, Tore Roaldsson's sister.' Torolv nodded towards their host.

Gunnhild cocked her head, waiting for him to continue.

'As Tora's father was long dead, Bjørn sought out Tore to ask for his sister's hand. But Tore refused, no matter what Bjørn said.'

'Why? You said he was wealthy.'

'There is more to a man than his wealth. But Tore never spoke to me about it, so I can only guess at his motives. Perhaps he thought Bjørn was too eager and impressed with himself?'

Gunnhild smiled. 'I know the kind.'

Torolv laughed. 'I guess you do! But Bjørn left Svanøy without any agreement with Tore and would not accept his refusal. So one day, when Tore was away, Bjørn returned and took Tora back to his farm in Sogn.'

'Without Tore's blessing?'

Torolv affirmed with a solemn nod. 'Brynjolf, Tore's friend and Bjørn's father, was incensed by his son's impudence. He dispatched emissaries to Tore to negotiate amends for his son's brash actions. Tore demanded the return of Tora, but Bjørn stubbornly refused to relinquish her. A harsh winter passed, filled with tension. When summer arrived, Bjørn and Tora escaped to the west, visiting Shetland, Orkney and Dublin. But they were outlawed in Norway, and they found themselves on the run. In desperation, they sought refuge in Iceland at my father's estates at Borg. Upon learning the young woman's identity, my father warmly welcomed the sister of his childhood companion.'

'Of course! Your father grew up with Tore as his foster brother!'

'Indeed. Imagine the fury that gripped Skallagrim upon discovering Bjørn had claimed Tora without Tore's blessing. He seethed with the desire to slay Bjørn for his treachery and deceit, but my mother and I succeeded in pacifying him. Instead, we turned our efforts towards mediating a resolution between Tore and Brynjolf. The ensuing months saw an unending exchange of messengers. During this time, Tora birthed a daughter, Asgerd, within our household. Once Tore consented to their return to Norway, Tora, out of fear for her infant's safety on the sea voyage, decided to leave Asgerd in Borg, under the caring watch of my mother. So it was, I sailed to Norway alongside Bjørn and Tora, pledging to shield them and assist in their negotiations with Tore.'

Gunnhild whispered a quiet lament, 'What a heart-wrenching decision for a young mother.'

'True, but rest assured, Asgerd will lack nothing under my mother's attentive care. And her parents were reconciled with Tore, and they were later lawfully married.'

'So, a joyous ending? And was it then you met Eirik?'

'Not entirely, and yes, in part. I've heard unfortunate news of Tora falling ill and passing on, leaving Bjørn a widower. Bjørn then took Alof Erlingsdotter as his wife, and they had a daughter together.' Torolv broke into a chuckle. 'Her name, as it happens, is Gunnhild.'

Gunnhild smiled.

'But, yes, it was on my first visit to Tore I found young Eirik admiring my ship. We've been friends ever since.'

'And now, you leave us?'

'Yes, I've been away for many years, only making a few brief visits to Borg. I greatly desire to speak with my father and seek my own adventures.'

'I shall miss you,' Gunnhild said.

'And I shall miss you. But soon, you will have a husband and children to look after, and you will not have the time to miss Torolv Skallagrimsson.'

'I'm not sure that is true,' Gunnhild said, and for a brief moment, she rested her head against his firm shoulder.

*

The next morning, they gathered on the pier to say goodbye to a dear friend.

After making the ship ready for the voyage to Iceland, Torolv Skallagrimsson jumped back to the pier and went to Eirik. They grabbed each other's massive forearms, exchanging petty insults in loud and unnaturally deep voices. Yet, there was no mistaking the sorrow on Eirik's face as he turned to Arinbjørn to take the gift he had prepared.

'Long have our families been at odds with each other,' Eirik said, as he turned back to Torolv, 'yet, you have proven a loyal friend since the first time we met. Therefore, I had this axe made for your father, Skallagrim, as a token of a renewed friendship between our houses. I did not expect the day of parting to come so soon.'

Eirik handed Torolv a large, snag-horned axe. It was gold-mounted, with the hilt overlaid with silver. It was truly a king's treasure.

Torolv graciously accepted the gift, before he said goodbye

to everyone on the pier, except Gunnhild, with whom he exchanged the briefest of smiles. They'd agreed it would be unwise to show their affection in front of everyone.

Besides, they said their goodbyes the night before.

The moment Torolv jumped back on his ship, Eirik turned on his heel.

'Come, Arinbjørn! We have plans to make!'

CHAPTER: DEPARTURE

Svanøy, Firdafylke

As Eirik, Arinbjørn and the remaining throng made their way back to the grand hall, Gunnhild found herself rooted in her spot, her eyes fixated on the receding ship. The clear morning sunlight glinted off the ship's carvings and painted shields, making it shimmer against the tranquil sea.

The brevity of their time together did little to mitigate the sharp pang of her friend's absence. Memories of laughter shared, stories swapped, and stolen intimate moments now filled her with a deep, echoing ache. With Torolv's departure, these memories and the heavy weight of loss were all she had left.

As Gunnhild continued her watch, she thought of her future. Her engagement with Eirik would soon lead to marriage, bringing a new set of responsibilities. She thought of the children they would have, and the life they would build together. Eirik was a man worthy of respect, a future king, and she knew that he would treat her with kindness. Yet, part of her heart still ached for what could have been.

Sighing deeply, she allowed herself one last look at Torolv's ship, now merely a speck against the vastness of the sea, before turning back to the hall. There was work to be done, preparations to be made for her wedding, and the rest of her life waiting for her.

Gunnhild stood on the precipice of an uncertain future,

but she resolved to meet it with the same strength and courage she always had. In her heart, she harboured hopes for Torolv, of the possibility of their paths crossing again someday.

, Back at the hall, Eirik and Arinbjørn were deep in conversation, their heads huddled together as they looked over a parchment. As Gunnhild approached, Eirik looked up, a smile spreading across his face.

'There you are, Gunnhild! We've been waiting for you. Come, join us. We have much to discuss.'

Gunnhild drew a deep breath, forcing a smile on to her face as she moved to occupy the seat beside her betrothed.

CHAPTER: HARALD FAIRHAIR

Avaldsnes, Rogaland

Trailing her future husband across the king's farm at Avaldsnes, Gunnhild shrank under the weight of unseen gazes. Servants, thralls and hirdmen paused to acknowledge Eirik, their interactions brief and largely silent. But for her, there were no greetings, no recognition. She was the outsider here.

Torolv's tale about how the callous Harald Fairhair had murdered his uncle echoed in her head as they came ever closer to meeting the infamous king who had forced the whole of Norway under his oppressive rule. It was difficult to imagine a stronger contrast from her previous life with the two noaidis in a hut in Finnmark.

What would Fairhair say when he learnt about her past life? Would the ambitious king allow his heir to marry a woman of an insignificant lineage, from a remote part of the realm? Would he order her executed for practising sorcery?

She almost tripped as she walked through the door. The shadows inside welcomed her, concealed her, and allowed her to breathe again.

'My lord king,' said a man's voice, 'your son, Eirik, and his betrothed, Gunnhild Ossutsdotter of Håløygaland.'

Gunnhild looked up at the middle-aged man, utterly nondescript except for his fine garments.

Who was he, and how did he know about her?

'Thank you, Kjartan. You may leave us.'

Gunnhild dared to look up, just enough to cast a glance at the man in the high seat.

King Harald Fairhair was an imposing figure. His posture was erect, and he exuded the strength and determination of a much younger man. There was a regal air to his appearance, with wrinkles etched on his face and a crown of white hair.

Behind the throne hung a dozen painted shields and two large tapestries depicting battles. *His* battles, Gunnhild surmised.

'Come closer, both of you,' the king said, with the confident tone of one who was absolutely certain to be obeyed.

Gunnhild tried to walk steadily on the thick, lavish rugs as they approached the throne on the raised dais. Despite the lingering scent of roasted meat and baked bread from a previous meal, there was a hint of old-man's odour. The hand resting on the armrest trembled slightly, but his eyes were still sharp and alert.

'Welcome back, Eirik,' the king said. 'Did you enjoy Bjarmeland?'

'They offered stern resistance, and we lost a handful of good men. But it was a profitable journey,' Eirik replied.

Gunnhild sensed a tension between father and son, a tone of formality she suspected was there because of her.

'So I see,' the king said, looking at Gunnhild.

'My king,' Eirik said, upholding the uncomfortable formality, 'this is Gunnhild Ossutsdotter of Håløygaland, my betrothed and future queen.'

'I see. It's a pleasure to gaze upon you with my own eyes, Gunnhild. Your reputation precedes you,' the king said.

'Thank you, my king,' she replied hesitantly, unsure of which reputation the king was referring to.

The king chuckled. 'Has your father given his consent to your becoming Eirik's wife?'

'He has,' Gunnhild said, her voice flat.

'And you?'

Gunnhild held the king's gaze for a few heartbeats before she replied.

'It does not matter much how I feel about it, my king.'

'When your king asks about it, it does matter a great deal,' King Harald replied.

'I ask for your pardon, my king. Indeed, a woman could be less fortunate than to be betrothed to the throne's heir. Your son possesses strength and charm beyond most men. If he also learns to carry the wisdom of a grown man, I'll have no room for complaint.'

King Harald burst out laughing. Eirik gave her a feigned, stern look.

'Quick wits and a sharp tongue!' the king said. 'How you remind me ...'

After a brief pause, King Harald's expression changed, and he addressed Eirik.

'Now, let me hear how you intend to proceed.'

Eirik cleared his throat. 'I intend for us to spend the winter on Svanøy and plan the summer campaign. Torolv suggested Courland, but Arinbjørn favours Friesland. In either case, we need a stronger force. Five hundred men or more ...'

'Stop,' said the king.

'As the resistance we face on our raids grows stronger, year by year. In Francia ...'

'Stop!'

Eirik stopped talking.

'You think and speak like a Viking, not a king. I have lived longer than most and ruled Norway for half a century. I feel my body and mind withering. Soon, I will pass on, and it will be your responsibility to rule the whole of Norway as a king.'

'I will, when the time comes,' Eirik said.

'The time is now!' the king rebuked.

Eirik held his silence.

'Now is the time to start acting as a king, not a child chasing the next thrill.'

'And how does one do that?'

'If you intend to marry Gunnhild, you will do so now. And you shall spend the winter visiting every hersir, jarl and wealthy farmer you can find. A king cannot survive without allies. I had planned for you to marry the daughter of King Gorm of Denmark, but that is no longer an option. In choosing Ossut Tote's daughter as your queen, you instead gain influence over Håløygaland and the northern trade routes, previously dominated by the jarls of Lade.'

'I understand,' Eirik said.

'Good,' the king said. 'We shall make the necessary arrangements for your wedding, here at Avaldsnes, before the last day of summer.'

Eirik nodded.

'One more thing,' the king said. 'From the day the two of you are married, you shall use the titles *king* and *queen*, on every occasion. You are bound to the realm, and the realm is bound to you.'

'I understand,' said Eirik.

'Now leave us, so that I may have a word in private with my daughter-in-law.'

Gunnhild felt a surge of trepidation. She desperately wanted Eirik to refuse, to protect her from whatever this intimidating king had in store for her.

But, alas, Eirik turned on his heel and stomped out of the great hall without as much as a backward glance.

CHAPTER: MOTHER OF KINGS

Under the flickering light of a nearby torch, King Harald turned to Gunnhild, a stern seriousness etching his hardened features. 'I wanted to talk to you, Gunnhild,' he began, his voice low and grating. 'Not because you are my future daughter-in-law, but because you will be the mother of kings. Norway's future depends on how you play your part.'

Gunnhild, taken aback by his forthright words, managed to keep a composed facade. 'You flatter me, my king,' she responded, a trace of uncertainty lacing her words.

Harald, his gaze unyielding, shook his head slightly. 'That was not my intention,' he asserted, his voice echoing in the vast, empty hall. 'I fought for many years to unify Norway under my rule, and I have named Eirik as my heir. But one weak link might break the chain. If you don't provide him with sons, the realm will once again be ruled by Danes, jarls and petty kings.'

'And now your son and heir finds himself a bride from the far north, when he should have married the daughter of a wealthy jarl or a Danish king.'

Harald laughed. 'Perhaps, and I will admit that was my first thought when I heard about you. But Eirik might have stumbled upon a clever decision. Håløygaland is a vast region, rich in trade goods. For generations, ever since Grjotgard travelled south from Andøy and settled in Trøndelag, the profits from the northern trade have filled the coffers of the jarl of Lade. If your marriage can extend Eirik's influence north to

Håløygaland, it might consolidate his position.'

'Perhaps,' said Gunnhild.

'Besides, Eirik's mother was Ragnhild Eiriksdatter of Hedeby. If my son also married the daughter of a Danish king, his sons would be more Danish than Norwegian.'

'I understand,' Gunnhild said, and looked up to meet King Harald's eyes. 'May I speak frankly, my king?'

Harald looked surprised. A slight smile played in the corner of his mouth when he nodded. 'Of course. How could I trust you if you didn't?'

'Thank you, my king,' Gunnhild said. 'Why do you say Eirik is your heir?'

'Because I have named him my heir,' King Harald's eyes narrowed.

'How, and when?'

'On the Eidsivating, the year after Ragnhild died.'

'When was this?'

Harald grimaced. 'Some twenty winters ago.'

'Do you think everybody agreed with your decision?'

'That is of no consequence! I am the king, and my word is law.'

'Your word is nothing, my king,' Gunnhild stated, her voice steady despite the audacity of her words.

'What is this? I invited you to speak frankly, but this is pure insolence! I believe this meeting has run its course,' Harald said, and rose from his seat.

'As long as you live, your words are backed by your armies, your gold and your alliances! Take those away, and your words are just … words,' Gunnhild pressed on.

King Harald froze and locked eyes with her. After a tense moment, he lowered himself back on to his seat, the heavy wooden chair groaning under his weight.

Gunnhild felt compelled to say something that might break the tension.

'Why is Eirik your heir, my king?' Gunnhild asked, her tone softer.

'His mother was the love of my life. I divorced my other wives when I married Ragnhild Eiriksdatter.'

'How many wives did you have?'

'Eight.'

'Eight?' Gunnhild could not hide her surprise.

'Or eleven, depending on how you count.' King Harald looked tired.

'I see. How many sons do you have?'

'Two dozen, at least. I haven't tried counting them lately. I've travelled a lot and met many women. If a man claims he's my son, I can't really prove him wrong.'

'It's easier for women to keep track of their offspring, I suppose,' Gunnhild offered.

Harald smiled. 'Thank you.'

'But when you die, Eirik will have twenty brothers contending for the throne?'

'Some of them are dead, and not all of those who live would have such ambitions,' King Harald protested.

'Who would be Eirik's most important rivals?'

Harald sighed. 'Well, my first wife was Åsa, the daughter of Jarl Håkon of Lade. I have four sons with her. My firstborn, Guttorm, ruled in Viken until he was slain by Solve Klove years ago. The twins and Sigrød now rule in Trøndelag. They would be fierce enemies. Trøndelag is wealthy and renowned for its warriors.'

'Do they have names, your twins?'

'Halvdan.'

'And?'

'Halvdan.'

'Surely not!'

Harald shrugged. 'Halvdan the Black and Halvdan the White.'

Gunnhild shook her head in disbelief. 'Who else?'

'My next wife was Gyda, daughter of King Eirik of Hordaland who I slew at the battle of Hafrsfjord. By Gyda, I have Rørek and Sigtrygg. I don't expect either of them to challenge for the throne. The two youngest, Frode and Torgils, died in Ireland. Our daughter Ålov married Jarl Tore Teiande, son of my old friend, Ragnvald Mørejarl.'

'That makes eight, including those who are dead,' Gunnhild said.

'With Åshild, daughter of Ring Dagsson of Ringerike, I have three sons: Dag and Ring, who rule Hedemark and Gudbrandsdal; and Gudrød, whose estate is not far from here.'

'What do you mean when you say your sons *rule* those regions?'

'The eldest of my sons serve as underkings.'

'What does that entail?'

'They have their own estates and collect taxes. But half their revenue goes to me, as the overking.'

'What happens if they don't pay you half of their revenue?'

Harald smiled. 'Then I will have to bring my army and reason with my son.'

'Can you still do that if his army is larger than yours?'

'Nobody's army is larger than mine!'

'What if they combine their forces?'

'Why would they?' Harald frowned.

'To avoid giving away half their revenue.'

The king did not reply but looked at Gunnhild with a thoughtful expression.

'Eleven,' Gunnhild said.

'What?'

'Eleven sons. Who are the others?'

'Oh, well. There was Svanhild, daughter of Øystein Jarl. Our sons are Olav, ruler of Vingulmark, and Ragnar and Bjørn.'

'What can we expect from them?'

'Olav and Ragnar might cause problems for Eirik.'

'And Bjørn?'

'Bjørn Farmann is about your age, and he shows much promise. But he's a merchant, not a warrior.'

'Fourteen.'

Harald sighed. 'And then there was Snøfrid.'

'Yes?'

For a moment, the king wavered. He looked away and swallowed a few times before he continued.

'Snøfrid was much like you. Diminutive of body, but of unrivalled beauty. She was a sorceress of the Kvenir people. For years, all I could think of was her. To this day, I do not know if I was in love or enthralled by her spells.'

'I'm sorry,' Gunnhild said.

'Don't be. Those were my best years. At least, I thought so at the time.' After a pause, he added. 'Her sons were Sigurd Rise, Halvdan Hålegg, Gudrød Ljome and Ragnvald Rettilbeine, all as unruly as their mother.'

'Were?'

'Only two remain. Sigurd rules over Ringerike, and Ragnvald over Hadeland. Gudrød drowned, and Halvdan was slain on the Orkneys.'

Gunnhild nodded thoughtfully.

'And there is Tora Mostaff's son, Haakon,' Harald said with a smile. 'He's a bright boy and won't cause any problems.'

'Not yet, at any rate,' Gunnhild added. 'Are there more?'

'I've spent a lifetime visiting jarls, merchants and wealthy farmers, and I've shared beds with their daughters. I have dozens of sons and daughters, but I don't expect you to hear from them. Most are settled on large farms with enough land to live comfortable lives.'

'So, my future husband already has a dozen enemies?'

Harald laughed. 'Oh, no! He's far more enemies than that! Those are only his brothers. There are also the Danes in the south and the Gautar in the east. And a handful of hostile jarls, and all those who have fled to Iceland.'

'What can I possibly do to help Eirik keep his throne?'

'Give him sons. And stay close to him, lest he sires sons with other women. It would seem a king can have too many sons. And too many brothers.'

Gunnhild nodded gravely.

'When I grew up, I could always rely on the counsel of wiser men and women. First, there was my mother and my uncle Guttorm. Later, there was Håkon Ladejarl and Ragnvald Mørejarl, and many others. Eirik has always favoured action and warfare over patience and diplomacy, and his friends are as green as he is. Such kings might win glorious battles, but they rarely live long. He needs someone to temper him and talk some sense into him.'

'I shall do my best. Thank you, my king.'

CHAPTER: UNION

Avaldsnes, Rogaland

At the entrance of the dimly lit temple, Gunnhild stood, a knot of anticipation and doubt tightening in her heart. Her eyes trailed over the stern faces of the Norse gods, their carved visages casting long, brooding shadows in the flickering torchlight. The murmurs of the guests filled the air, a subtle reminder of the weight of the moment.

As the heavy doors swung open, Eirik Haraldsson, the man she was about to marry, strode in with confidence. The room fell into an uneasy silence, all eyes fixed on him. Gunnhild's gaze met Eirik's, but her mind could not escape her longing for Torolv, the man who had stirred conflicting emotions within her.

The *goði* stepped forward to officiate the ceremony. Dressed in a sacred garb and carrying a staff inscribed with ancient runes, he represented the connection between mortals and the gods.

Amid the chanting and the scents of burning herbs, Eirik and Gunnhild partook in the sacred ritual of handfasting. Their forearms entwined, bound as one, and a stir of comfort and unease coursed through Gunnhild from Eirik's assertive grasp. Their eyes locked, and they exchanged their vows.

Gunnhild's voice quivered as she spoke, her words laced with her inner conflict.

'I, Gunnhild, daughter of Ossut Tote, pledge my heart and soul to you, Eirik Haraldsson. I vow to honour and cherish you as my husband, to stand by your side in times of joy and sorrow, to be your unwavering support. With each passing day, I promise to deepen our love and to nurture our union.'

Eirik, his voice resonating with strength and reverence, responded with fervour. 'I, Eirik Haraldsson, son of King Harald Halvdansson, pledge my heart and my sword to you, Gunnhild. I vow to protect you with all my might, to provide for you, and to shield you from harm. I will be your steadfast partner, your shelter in times of turmoil, and your guiding light in the darkest of days.'

The goði, witnessing their exchange, spoke firmly. 'May the gods bear witness and bless this union. May your bond grow strong and endure the tests of time.'

With their vows acknowledged, Eirik and Gunnhild exchanged rings, symbolising their commitment. The goði blessed the rings and raised their hands, invoking the blessings of the gods upon Eirik and Gunnhild. The gathered assembly joined in the chants, their voices echoing through the temple.

With the sacred rites complete, the newlyweds, alongside their guests, sauntered from the temple to the great hall. A grand feast lay in wait, its abundance spilling over the tables in a breathtaking display. Platters piled high with succulent cuts of meat—lamb, boar and venison—were surrounded by bowls brimming with steaming vegetables and hearty stews. Cups were filled to the brim with mead and ale, their golden hues shimmering in the warm light. The air was filled with the tantalising aroma of roasting meats mingling with the sweet scent of freshly baked bread.

Eirik and Gunnhild settled into their seats at the head of the grand table, the weight of her doubts hanging heavy in the air. Gunnhild took a deep breath, her voice quivering as she finally voiced her concerns.

'Eirik, there is unease within my heart,' she confessed, a tremble in her voice. 'Yet your strength and sincerity offer solace. Would you grant me time, that affection may grow?'

Eirik's features softened, his hand reaching out to ensnare hers. 'Gunnhild, my queen, your love is not my command. Together, we shall carve our path.'

These words, though modest, sparked a glimmer of hope within Gunnhild's heart. She took a deep breath and replied, 'Then let us embrace this union, Eirik, and make the best of it— for our sake and the sake of our realm.'

PART TWO

Egil Skallagrimsson

CHAPTER: RAGNVALD RETTILBEINE

Avaldsnes, Rogaland, 925

'My lord Eirik,' Kjartan, King Harald's steward, said and bowed. 'The king invites the prince and princess to a council in his chambers.'

'Now?' Eirik replied. 'We were just about to ... go to bed.'

'Yes, I noticed,' Kjartan said. 'And that's why I made such an effort to be polite about it. But the king was quite insistent on seeing the two of you.'

'My father can never wait for anything,' Eirik complained while he looked for his finer garments.

'Ha!' said Gunnhild, half muffled as she pulled an embroidered linen dress over her head. 'Fortunately, his son is not like him at all.'

Eirik turned to Kjartan. 'Gunnhild, too? Are you sure?'

Kjartan just bowed again. The stewards had picked up all sorts of foreign customs from Denmark, Francia and England.

Moments later, Eirik and Gunnhild hurried over to the farmyard to King Harald's longhouse. Kjartan held the door open, bowed as they entered, and closed it behind them.

'I've slain a dozen monks far manlier than that one,' Eirik grunted once they were inside.

Gunnhild smirked, her tone dripping with sarcasm. 'You are such a brave warrior.'

'That is not what I meant.'

'I know.'

'Welcome! Please join me here by the fire,' King Harald shouted from the other side of the hall. 'The nights have been so cold lately.'

'Good evening, Father,' Eirik said. 'You wanted to see us?'

'I did. But come here and sit down. I can hardly see you in the shadows.'

Eirik and Gunnhild shared a fleeting glance, a silent conversation in their gaze, as they traversed the expansive room, the echo of their footfalls the only sound. They found seats by the fireplace, the embers casting dancing shadows across their faces.

'There is beer, curd and whey on the table for you,' Harald said. 'I told the servants to leave us alone for this meeting.'

'Has something happened?' Gunnhild asked as she picked up a horn of beer and handed it to Eirik.

'Nothing for you?' Eirik asked.

'Not tonight,' Gunnhild said. 'I've not felt well lately.'

King Harald chuckled.

'What?' said Eirik.

'Oh, nothing.' Harald looked at Gunnhild and grinned.

Gunnhild's gaze hardened, her voice cool as she redirected the conversation. 'Why did you summon us, my king?'

'Ah, well. Things have happened that the future king and queen should know about. And there are some unpleasant affairs that must be dealt with,' said Harald.

'Let's hear it,' said Eirik.

'I've sent your brother to Aethelstan,' Harald revealed, a spark of conspiracy in his eyes.

'Which brother?'

'Who do you think? Haakon, of course!'

Eirik shrugged.

'Why Aethelstan, and not Tora's kin in Moster?' said Gunnhild.

Harald's gaze turned distant, a wry smile creeping on to his face. 'Let's just say that I've reached an understanding with Aethelstan, and Haakon is now a crucial part of that understanding.'

'There is more to that story,' Gunnhild said.

'There is,' said Harald, 'but please let an old man take some secrets to his grave. Suffice to say that Haakon will get a thorough education at Aethelstan's court. Perhaps the king might even name him as his jarl.'

'In England?' said Eirik.

'Northumbria,' said Harald. 'The north is swarming with Norwegians and Danes, and they usually prefer to be ruled by one of their own rather than a king in the south.'

'Well, thank you, Father,' said Eirik. 'I shall sleep sounder knowing there is one less brother vying for the throne. Was there anything else?'

'Yes, and this is a less pleasant matter,' said Harald. 'It concerns Ragnvald.'

Eirik grimaced. 'Your friend Ragnvald is dead, Father.'

'Not Ragnvald Mørejarl! I'm talking about my son, Ragnvald Rettilbeine!'

'Snøfrid?' asked Gunnhild.

'Yes!' Harald looked at her and nodded approvingly. 'The offspring of my love affair with Snøfrid. Well, one of them.'

'The sorceress?' asked Eirik.

Harald's voice boomed, echoing off the stone walls. 'She was my wife!'

'She was your mistress, not your wife,' Eirik interjected, his gaze drifting away from Harald. 'Her sorcerous influence lingered even a year after her death. The whole realm feasts on tales of your scandalous affair with the sorceress.'

Harald slumped down in his seat. 'I know, and that's why this is a matter of the gravest importance. Her son, Ragnvald, considers himself a seiðmann. He lives and travels the land in the company of half a hundred other seiðmenn and sorcerers. They practise their dark arts and lie with each other, all the while announcing to the world, he is Harald Fairhair's son and heir to the throne. He has become quite a thorn in our side.'

Harald leaned forward in his seat.

'Earlier this summer, my people complained about a seiðmann named Vitgeir who practised in Hordaland. The farmers were concerned about the seiðmann cursing their crops and their livestock. One of my hersirs had lost a son to fever three days after he had asked Vitgeir to leave. I sent a messenger and asked him to abandon his vile sorcery or leave my realm. Vitgeir replied with a verse':

'The danger surely is not great.

From seiðmenn born of mean estate,

When Harald's son in Hadeland,

King Ragnvald, to the art lays hand.'

After this recital, Harald met his son's gaze in silence.

Eirik looked back at him and blinked a few times. 'What do you expect me to do with this information?'

'I believe your father is suggesting it's time to tighten your grip on the throne, Eirik,' Gunnhild said.

CHAPTER: ASGJERD

Svanøy, Firdafylke

'Torolv! It's good to see you back!' Arinbjørn's voice echoed from the pier, carried by the wind. Torolv, standing on the prow of the approaching ship, waved back.

Arinbjørn eyed the vessel, a merchant ship by his estimate, with room enough for about sixteen men. Certainly not a ship meant for a Viking raid.

'Look at you,' Torolv said as he jumped on to the pier. 'You almost look like a man! How long has it been?'

'Three winters have passed since you left,' Arinbjørn said. 'You look well, like a man who's found a fortune.'

Torolv laughed. 'Your eyes are sharp, my friend. There are many tales for another day. But let me introduce you to my travelling companions.'

Torolv turned back to the ship and gave a hand to a young woman climbing over the railing.

'Arinbjørn, this is Asgjerd Bjørnsdotter. Your cousin.'

'Nice to meet you, Arinbjørn,' Asgjerd said. 'I've heard much about you, and everything has been good.'

'Thank you, Asgjerd. It's a pleasure to see you after all those years. Is it your first visit to Norway?'

'Yes, I was born in Iceland, and I stayed behind at Borg when my parents returned to Norway. I'm looking forward to meeting my family.'

'Have you seen your father?' said Arinbjørn.

'Yes, we just came from there. He's doing well.'

'I'm sure he is,' Arinbjørn replied, his gaze lifting to catch sight of a dark-haired young man leaping on to the pier from behind Asgjerd. 'And you must be Egil Skallagrimsson.'

Egil stepped past Asgjerd, grabbed Arinbjørn's forearm, and shook it vigorously.

'Welcome to Svanøy, Egil and Asgjerd. Let me take you to my father. He will be delighted to meet members of his kin.'

The three guests from Iceland followed Arinbjørn the five hundred paces to Tore Roaldsson's longhouse.

'Father! Look what washed ashore this morning,' Arinbjørn shouted as they entered the hall.

Tore looked up from an almost empty plate and rose to greet the guests. 'Torolv! How good to see you! Have you stayed in Iceland all this time?'

Torolv laughed. 'Hardly! I've spent the summers raiding wherever the winds would take me. But during the winters, I've stayed at Borg with my family.'

'How is Skallagrim doing? It's been so long since I saw him,' said Tore.

'My father is still alive, as grumpy as ever,' Torolv replied.

'I'm glad to hear it,' Tore said and looked past Torolv's shoulder to other guests. 'And unless my eyes deceive me, this must be another of Skallagrim's sons.' Tore stepped past Torolv and grabbed Egil's forearm. 'I'm Tore Roaldsson. I grew up with your father on Kveldulv's farm.'

'A pleasure to meet you, Tore Roaldsson,' Egil said. 'My father speaks highly of you.'

'I'm pleased to hear that,' Tore said. 'I hope you will stay with us for some time. If you are anything like your brother, you will be a great asset while you're here.'

'Thank you,' said Egil. 'As you can see, I am nothing like my brother. But I will nevertheless consider your generous offer.'

Tore smiled and shook Egil's hand again.

'Now, allow me to introduce you to Asgjerd,' said Torolv. 'Your niece.'

Tore politely greeted Asgjerd before he looked back at Torolv with a questioning look.

'Asgjerd is the daughter of Bjørn Brynjolfsson and your sister Tora,' said Torolv. 'From their visit to Iceland.'

'An unfortunate adventure, that was,' Tore said and looked back at Asgjerd. 'But the child can hardly be blamed for her parent's poor judgement. Welcome to Svanøy, Asgjerd. It's a pleasure to meet you.'

'Thank you,' Asgjerd said.

'Well, I'm sure you're hungry and thirsty after your travels,' Tore said, and waved at a household servant. 'Please join me at the table.'

The guests accepted, and soon all five were talking and catching up on news from Norway, Iceland and many other places. Tore settled for a large horn of beer while the others enjoyed a generous selection of bread, meat, cheeses, vegetables and fruits.

'Thank you for this tasty meal, Tore,' said Torolv. 'From what I find on your table and what I saw on my way to your longhouse, you must be a prosperous man. Even more so than three winters ago. Have you made any more investments lately?'

'You have an eye for details, Torolv,' Tore replied. 'Indeed, some of my ventures have prospered in recent years. My quarries, in particular. There seems to be an endless demand for millstones.'

'To millstones!' Torolv said and held his beer horn aloft.

'Millstones!' the others chimed in and emptied their horns.

Tore wiped his mouth and spoke.

'And what about yourself, Torolv? You've spent half your

life looking for adventure wherever you could find it, and you own fast ships, sharp weapons and fine clothes. Will there come a day when you settle down and start a family of your own?'

A wide grin stretched across Torolv's face. 'I'm glad you've asked, for it's precisely one of the reasons I've made my way here,' he declared.

'Is that so,' Tore said. 'What did you have in mind?'

Torolv rose and cleared his throat. 'You mentioned the unfortunate adventures of Bjørn Brynjolfsson and your sister Tora Lacehand. As you know, but the younger among us might not have heard, Bjørn sought Tora's hand in marriage. The decision fell to you, as your father had passed away, and you refused. Bjørn returned in autumn, while you were away, and took Tora to his estate at Aurland. They married without your consent, and your sister spent the winter with Bjørn. In spring, they sailed from Norway, as the king had made Bjørn an outlaw. Eventually, they arrived at Borg in Iceland, and Asgjerd was born in our home. Bjørn and Tora returned after the winters in Iceland, when they were no longer outlaws, but Asgjerd remained with us.'

Torolv looked at young Asgjerd and smiled before he looked back at Tore.

'Now, I have spent the last three winters with young Asgjerd, and I've come to enjoy her company. So much that I want to ask you for her hand in marriage.'

Arinbjørn cast a quick glance at the others. Asgjerd looked down, with red cheeks and the slightest hint of a smile. Egil looked straight ahead at nobody. His face was stone. Tore looked from Torolv to Asgjerd, and back again.

'Well, as you say, Bjørn Brynjolfsson is Asgjerd's father. Though I appreciate your courtesy, it is not for me to give Asgjerd to you in marriage,' Tore said.

'That is true. Bjørn has already given his approval. But because of the story with Bjørn and your sister, I wanted to give you the right to consent to my marriage with Asgjerd. Or refuse if you are so inclined,' Torolv said.

Tore looked at Asgjerd for some time before he replied.

'I thank you for this courtesy. From what I can tell, Asgjerd is not opposed to becoming your wife. For what my opinion is worth in this matter, I give you my approval,' Tore said.

Torolv smiled from ear to ear as he shook Tore's arm. Arinbjørn congratulated Asgjerd, then Torolv.

'I thank you, Tore Roaldsson,' said Torolv. 'And I hereby invite you and your family to our wedding two weeks from now, on Bjørn's estate in Aurland.'

Arinbjørn turned to see Egil Skallagrimsson walking out of the hall without a word.

CHAPTER: ATLØY

Atløy, Firdafylke

The howling wind tore at their sodden clothes as Eirik, Gunnhild and their retinue arrived at Eirik's farm on Atløy, managed by the diligent and reliable Bård. For a week, they had sailed and trudged through relentless wind and rain, moving from one farm to another, their spirits as drenched as their clothes. Gunnhild could sense in her bones that the weather would improve, and she looked forward to two days and nights in the comfort of Bård's longhouse.

Gunnhild cradled her swelling belly, the evidence of her condition now impossible to hide. With a weary yet resolute voice, she had whispered to Eirik, 'This journey will be my last before our child arrives.'

They were invited to a *blót*, with sacrifices to the guardian spirits, and the promise of abundant food and drink. Servants greeted them in the farmyard, helped them inside, and offered dry clothes, woollen blankets, and warm milk.

After some time, the guests were quite comfortable, and their host's absence was conspicuous.

'Where is Bård, your master?' King Eirik asked one of the more senior servants.

'My apologies, my king,' the servant replied, his voice trembling. 'Master Bård is attending to other guests outside.'

'Who are these guests?' asked the king. 'Who could be more important to your master than us, requiring him to be outside rather than here, serving us?'

The servant bent so low his forehead almost touched the floor. 'I'm very sorry, my king. Olve, Tore Hersir's tax collector, arrived earlier today, along with half a dozen men.'

'Olve and Tore Hersir's men are my men!' the king exclaimed. 'Go fetch them at once and tell them to join us.'

And so it was done, and soon Bård, Olve and a handful of housecarls entered the great hall. They looked damp and disgruntled, but King Eirik greeted Olve and invited him to sit in the high seat facing him.

The man sitting beside Olve, directly across from Gunnhild, drew her attention. His height almost rivalled Eirik's, and his broad build resembled a wall of stone. His youthful aura belied an indecipherable age, and his stern demeanour cast an intimidating shadow. Every part of him—his chest, shoulders, even his robust face—projected a daunting breadth, a presence that Gunnhild found both repellent and captivating.

Being in his presence felt like being near an evil spirit. His darkness went beyond mere appearance. She could feel his depth, or rather, she couldn't help but feel it. It was like a cold, black cloud enveloping her, seeping into her, and darkening her mind. Death shadowed this stranger, ready to pounce at anyone who stood in his path. She glanced down at her clenched hands and the goosebumps on her arms and pulled her sleeves down to conceal her reaction.

Gunnhild resisted the urge to ask Eirik who this stranger was. His foul spirit told her all she needed to know, and neither name nor lineage could was that away.

Her sense of foreboding did not improve with time. With every toast, with every horn of ale, Olve's companions drank themselves senseless. Some ran out to vomit, others vomited inside. Bård worked hard to refill the drinking horns, while his servants did their best to clean up after them.

Only the dark-haired brute seemed to hold his drink well. Once, he took the horn Bård offered to Olve, and drained it.

'My apologies, Egil,' Bård said. 'I did not realise you were so thirsty! Here, let me get you another horn.'

Bård signalled to a maid, who hastened to give another full horn to the man known as Egil.

Egil took the horn and recited a stave:

'Wizard-worshipper of cairns!
Want of ale thou couldst allege,
Here at spirits' holy feast.
False deceiver thee I find.
Stranger guests thou didst beguile,
Cloaking thus thy churlish greed.
Bård, a miser base art thou,
Treacherous trick on such to play.'

Bård's face reddened. 'Cease your mockery. You're in the presence of the king and queen!'

Egil glanced at Gunnhild, then shrugged. He emptied his horn and held it out to be refilled.

Bård filled the horn without a word, although his clenched jaw revealed his emotions. He offered more ale to Olve and King Eirik before he came to Gunnhild.

'Would you like more to drink, my queen?' Bård said. He leaned closer to her and whispered, 'Perhaps my queen might know a remedy for such disgraceful behaviour?'

Gunnhild allowed their host to fill her horn, although the mere smell of ale brought a wave of nausea in her current state. Her discomfort, however, was primarily provoked not by the strong drink, but by the disruptive presence of the ominous figure looming among them. There was a brazen arrogance to his bearing, a blatant disregard for the social norms that governed such feasts. It was as if he were a wolf among dogs, and that wolfish nature didn't go unnoticed.

Her reaction was deeply instinctual, an overwhelming sense of caution unrelated to logic or rationality. The twin forces of fear and foreboding got the better of her, and she said,

'Have a servant gather three plants of northern water hemlock, roots included, and cleanse them thoroughly of earth and grime. When next you offer to refill my drink, I shall decline. Shortly thereafter, I will discreetly excuse myself and meet you outdoors. Bring with you the plants, a knife, a whetstone, and a horn filled with ale,' she whispered, her voice steadier than her pounding heart.

Bård's eyes widened for a moment, but he acted as instructed, and they soon met in the nearby brewhouse. Nestled on the edge of the farmstead, the brewhouse was a humble structure of timber and thatch, emanating a yeasty scent of fermenting ale. Inside the dimly lit interior, the flickering light of a single torch painted wavering shadows on the rough-hewn walls.

'Who is he?' Gunnhild asked once the door was shut behind them.

'An Icelander,' Bård replied with a shrug, 'by the name of Egil. One of Olve's men.'

Gunnhild nodded. There was more to the Icelander than Bård could tell her. She turned to scrutinising the plants Bård had gathered, holding them up against the meagre light, her face a mask of concentration. After a moment of intense examination of their tangled roots and serrated leaves, she nodded approvingly, deeming them suitable for the task ahead.

'This will cause him to vomit at first, like his companions inside. But next, comes the watery bowels, forcing him to withdraw. When he's alone, he will suffer from convulsions and breathlessness ...'

Bård's eyes widened as he watched her deftly manipulate the roots and lower stems of the hemlock. With deliberate strokes of a knife against a whetstone, she crushed the plant, extracting its lethal sap, which slowly dripped into the ale horn. Once she deemed it sufficient, she removed the remnants of the hemlock from the ale horn with a swift yank, disposing of them into the chilling night air outside.

'Discard these afterwards, and make sure you wash thoroughly lest you suffer the same fate,' she said. 'Now, where can I rinse my hands in running water?'

Bård showed her a small brook, just thirty paces from the longhouse, and went inside through the back door. As Gunnhild had predicted, the storm had passed, leaving nothing more than a refreshing drizzle. She returned to her seat just as a maid handed Egil the prepared ale horn.

Egil held the horn to his mouth, then stopped. His forehead wrinkled, making him look even more like an enraged ox. He drew his knife and pricked the palm of his hand. With the tip of the blade, he scratched some runes into the horn. Then, he smeared his blood on them and sang:

'Write we runes around the horn,
Redden all the spell with blood;
Wise words choose I for the cup
Wrought from branching horn of beast.
Drink we then, as drink we will.
Draught that cheerful bearer brings,
Learn that health abides in ale,
Holy ale that Bård hath blessed.'

Moments later, the horn burst asunder in the midst, and the ale was spilt on the straw below.

Bård hasted to fetch another horn of ale, to appease his troublesome guest. But before he could return, Egil rose to help Olve stand and find the door. The Icelander shifted his cloak to his left side just before they exited through the door. Bård ran after them with a full horn, and the door slammed shut behind them.

Gunnhild's worry grew as the three men stayed away longer than anticipated. Her thoughts churned with apprehension. She called over a maid, instructed her to find their host, and hoped her fear was merely unfounded anxiety.

The scream that tore from the maid as she opened the door confirmed her worst fears. An instant wave of chaos swept the longhouse as King Eirik and Olve's intoxicated men tried to muster their defences. It was a clumsy scramble more than a battle-ready response, with men falling over each other due to abrupt movement and others slipping in their own vomit.

With an air of authority, King Eirik managed to extricate himself from the confusion and was the first to step outside. When he returned, his hand was gripping his drawn sword and his stern face told a grim story.

'Bård is dead, and Olve is knocked out. Where is the big man who was sitting with Olve, the one who has been drinking more than any other?' The king's voice was harsh, his anger clear.

Amid the disoriented murmurs, a housecarl finally responded. 'He left with Olve a while ago.'

'Who is he?' the king demanded, his eyes surveying the room.

'An Icelander, my king. Egil Skallagrimsson,' answered the housecarl, voice wavering under the king's intense gaze.

A momentary grimace crossed King Eirik's face before he quickly hid it. His voice was firm and cold when he gave his command.

'Find him,' said the king, 'and bring him to me.'

Gunnhild felt a chill run down her spine at his words. She could not shake off the feeling that the night had spiralled into something far darker than she had anticipated.

CHAPTER: SAUDØY

Svanøy, Firdafylke

Arinbjørn turned at the sound of the subtle cough and found Haldor, his father's servant, waiting for an opportunity to speak.

Tore noticed him as well. 'Yes, Haldor?'

'My lord,' said Haldor, 'Olve has returned, and he wants to speak with you as soon as possible.'

Tore looked at Arinbjørn, then Torolv Skallagrimsson. Both shrugged.

'Send him in and tell the maids to bring food and drink for him,' said Tore.

Moments later, a dejected Olve entered Tore Hersir's great hall.

'My lord,' Olve began, his voice heavy, 'I come with bad news.'

'Join us, Olve. Eat while you share your story,' Tore replied, gesturing towards the feast.

Olve found a seat opposite Arinbjørn. He did not even look at Torolv. A maid brought him a horn of ale, which he declined with a peculiar grimace. He grabbed a piece of cheese and gulped it down before he could no longer hold back.

'My lord, Atløy-Bård is dead.' Olve stared at the cheese in his hand.

'Dead? What happened?' Tore exclaimed and rose to stand by the table.

Olve quickly dropped the cheese and rose. 'My lord, he was slain.'

'By whom?' Tore reached for a sword that did not hang on his hip. It rarely did, and never when he was enjoying a meal in his own hall.

'There was a drunken brawl, and Bård was slain by a man in our company.'

'Who?' Tore all but shouted.

'Egil Skallagrimsson, my lord,' Olve said, with a quick glance at Torolv.

Tore also looked at Torolv, who sat motionless with a grave expression. He motioned for Olve to join them. 'Tell me what happened.'

'When we first got there,' began Olve, 'we were weary and drenched from battling a storm at sea. Bård only offered curd and whey, claiming he had no ale or mead. We were disappointed but believed him. But when King Eirik and the queen came, and we joined the feast, we found out Bård did have plenty of ale—he just didn't want to share it with us! Egil was most disgruntled by this, and he made no effort to conceal his disdain for Atløy-Bård. Some of us drank more ale than we should—me included—and Egil most of all. Mean words were exchanged, and at some point Egil drove his sword through Bård while they were outside.'

Tore and Arinbjørn looked to Torolv, who nodded solemnly. 'Yes, this sounds just like my little brother.'

'Where is he now?' Tore asked.

'Nobody knows,' said Olve. 'On King Eirik's orders, we searched all night without finding him. We only learnt that he had taken his helmet, spear and shield with him when he fled. The next day, a search party of twelve housecarls landed on the nearby island of Saudøy. Egil must have swum there the night before, for he slew two of the king's men and maimed a third, before he escaped with their boat. Nobody has seen him since.

Despite what has happened, I expected him to return here, as there is nowhere else for him to go in this land.'

The four men spoke at length about what had happened and tried to guess where Egil might have fled. Torolv spent most of the evening staring down at his cup. After nightfall, he inhaled deeply and spoke.

'My brother is strong and clever, as good a skald as a warrior. But he is quick to anger and holds a grudge longer than anyone else—even in my family. In his third summer, he stole a horse and rode in the night to attend a feast. At eight, he split his friend's skull with a two-handed axe. At twelve, he slew a grown man—a man dear to our father. A mighty ally is Egil, and the most dangerous enemy.'

With that, Torolv rose and went to bed.

*

A knock on the door woke Arinbjørn up at dawn. The night had been too short, and his body resisted every attempt at getting out of bed.

'My lord, your father requires your presence in the great hall.' Arinbjørn recognised the maid's voice.

'Thank you, Astrid. I shall be there shortly. Give me some water to wash my face.'

The door creaked open, revealing Astrid holding a bowl filled with steaming water. Trailing behind her, Sigrid, her younger sister, carried a sizable mug of refreshing, cold water.

'A drink of water might do you some good as well,' Astrid teased, a playful spark in her eyes as she and her sister exited, leaving Arinbjørn in silence once more.

Shortly thereafter, Arinbjørn entered the grand hall. His father, Tore, detached himself from his imposing seat and made his way towards him. A shadowy figure was hunched over a plate at the far end of the long table, almost swallowed by the gloom.

'You've come quickly, Arinbjørn,' Tore acknowledged, a hint of gratitude in his tone. 'Let's wait for Torolv. Please, take a seat.'

As Arinbjørn bypassed his father, a flicker of recognition sparked in his mind—the figure was none other than Egil Skallagrimsson. He paused abruptly, his heart hammering in his chest, and Tore placed a soothing hand on his shoulder.

'Steady yourself, son,' Tore advised, his voice a low rumble. 'We'll navigate through this situation. Let's converse and unravel as much as we can, for now.' Arinbjørn found a seat opposite Egil, and he watched the huge man devour his food for a while. The intense odour, and the ale he consumed the night before, prevented him from developing any appetite.

'Hungry?'

Egil looked up and nodded. 'Yes.'

'You reek.'

Egil looked up and nodded. 'Yes.'

Arinbjørn gave up and asked the maid for another cup of fresh water. Tore kept his distance. Because of the stench, Arinbjørn guessed.

Soon, the door burst open, and Torolv Skallagrimsson entered the hall.

'For such a clever man, you can be quite a dimwit!' Torolv shouted as he strode towards his brother.

Egil stood and retorted, 'For a proclaimed simpleton, your cleverness surprises me!'

They approached each other for a fraternal embrace, but Torolv recoiled at the last second.

'By the gods! Did you bathe in dung before breakfast?' he asked, a grimace forming on his face.

'It was a cold night. I sought warmth among the livestock,' Egil confessed without a hint of embarrassment.

'Sounds like something you'd do,' Torolv replied with a

sigh, manoeuvring his way around the table to settle next to Arinbjørn. 'But tell me, how did you manage to escape Saudøy?'

Egil reclined back into his chair, inhaled deeply, and then recited with a dramatic flourish:

'From the clutches of Norway's king,
from the craft of Gunnhild,
I freed myself,
making no claims of courage.
Three men, known only to myself,
loyal warriors of the king,
now dwell in death's domain,
ushered to the hall of Hel.'

Arinbjørn, nodding to the rhythm of the verse, commended, 'Spoken like a true skald.'

Egil's lips curved into a sly smirk. 'I rowed for two full days and a night. Time aplenty for crafting verse.'

'That's indeed commendable,' Torolv noted, 'especially given your recent inability to attend my wedding due to sickness.'

Without raising his gaze to meet his brother's, Egil simply replied, 'I recovered.'

Tore Hersir interrupted the brothers' bickering. 'I've heard enough. It will be the common verdict that Atløy-Bård got more or less what he deserved for his deception. Yet, too eager is Egil Skallagrimsson to rekindle the flame of strife and brave a king's wrath—which most men find a heavy burden. However, I will go with Arinbjørn and do what I can to atone you with the king— for this time.'

CHAPTER: ATONEMENT

Askøy, Hordaland

Arinbjørn and Tore made their way to King Eirik and his hird, ensconced in the rugged majesty of Berg-Onund's estate at Fenring, halfway between Svanøy and Avaldsnes. The farm was surrounded by a meticulously constructed wooden palisade, a testament to the craftsmanship of its builders. The main gate, adorned with intricately carved dragon heads, opened to an expansive courtyard. At the heart of the estate stood a sizable longhouse, its tar-stained planks weathered by countless winters. Surrounding the longhouse were several outbuildings, including barns, a smithy and a stable. Each structure was well maintained and fit seamlessly into the overall layout of the estate.

After the pleasant greetings and exchange of news, Arinbjørn let his former brother-in-arms know there was an urgent matter they must discuss with the king. Without further questioning, the host had his longhouse prepared for a council.

'Tore! Arinbjørn! What a pleasant surprise! What brings you to Hordaland?' said King Eirik.

'My king,' Tore said, 'you seem to be in a good mood. How does the queen fare?'

'Thank you, Tore. Gunnhild rests at Avaldsnes, and we've agreed she will give birth to our first child there. There is no place safer than my father's estates these days, and the midwives are experienced. As for me, I've spent most of the day training and sparring with my men, and I feel better than I have in a long time.'

Arinbjørn kept silent and allowed his father to handle this delicate matter.

'I'm pleased to hear that, my king,' Tore said. 'Unfortunately, I'm afraid what I have to say will dampen your mood.'

Tore was right. Even before he said another word, King Eirik's eyes darkened, and his brow furrowed. 'Speak!'

'A few days ago, Egil Skallagrimsson came to Svanøy,' said Tore, his voice calm and steady.

'Egil Skallagrimsson!' the king shouted. 'I'd hoped the vile creature had drowned, or at least returned to Iceland!'

Tore kept calm and let Eirik vent his rage.

As Arinbjørn quietly observed the king, Eirik's expression changed from rage to something resembling hope. His jaw relaxed, and his eyes sparkled.

'Ah, but surely you keep him locked up and guarded? He shall stand trial at the Gulating and be punished for his crimes!'

The king looked expectantly at his foster father for confirmation.

'No,' Tore declared, his voice firm. 'Egil and his brother, Torolv, remain at Svanøy, not as captives, but as my esteemed guests.'

'Then I shall send men to apprehend them both!' King Eirik spat. 'And you, Tore Roaldsson, my foster father, what am I to do with one who shelters an enemy of the king?'

'The king can, of course, do whatever he wants,' Tore said. 'But I came to offer an alternative to revenge and violence. A king who is quick to anger will soon run out of friends, and his reign will be short-lived.'

'How dare you lecture me on how to be a king?' Eirik's face

was as red as before.

'I know little of how to be a king,' Tore said, 'but I know much about people. Fear will only take you so far. An oppressed population will turn against their king at the first opportunity. One day, you will wake up in a burning longhouse, have an accident at sea or lead your army into an ambush.'

King Eirik's gaze held steady on Tore, his expression betraying the storm of thoughts within him. When he finally broke the silence, his voice was meek, a stark contrast to the previously thunderous tone,

'Be that as it may. There has been nothing but strife and deceit between our and Kveldulv's kin, and I shall not suffer another of their offspring in my realm.'

'And yet, Torolv, son of Skallagrim, son of Kveldulv, had proven his friendship and loyalty to you since you were a boy. Do you intend to put him on trial as well?'

Eirik's face contorted into an expression of agony, as it often did when faced with problems with no apparent solution.

'What do you suggest?' the king said, at last.

'I came to seek atonement,' Tore said, 'for your sake, as much as his. Name the fine, and I shall pay it on his behalf.'

Eirik closed his eyes, and his face gradually regained its natural colour.

'He killed three men and maimed a fourth,' he said.

Tore nodded and produced a leather pouch the size of a fist. 'Full wergilds for the two slain housecarls, double for Atløy-Bård, and half for the survivor with the maimed leg.'

Eirik looked from the pouch to Tore and back again. With a sigh, he took the pouch and pocketed it without examining its content.

'Though I accept some atonement, Egil shall not be long harboured in my realm. But for the sake of your intercession, Tore, I will accept a fine for this man.'

'Thank you, my king,' Tore said.

King Eirik nodded, and Arinbjørn and Tore turned to leave.

'Wait,' said the king.

'Of course, my king,' said Tore.

'Arinbjørn stays here. I want him by my side when I settle a dispute with one of my brothers.'

Arinbjørn and Tore looked at each other.

'Of course,' Arinbjørn said.

'As the king pleases,' said Tore, and he left the longhouse.

CHAPTER: SEID

Hadeland

A week later, Eirik brought four dozen warriors to the forest of Hadeland to punish his brother Ragnvald Rettilbeine for his sorcery. It was well past nightfall when they arrived at the farm the seiðmenn used for their vile practices.

Eirik's hand landed firmly on Arinbjørn's shoulder, his voice barely a whisper in the shrouded darkness. 'Take a dozen men around the back. Your shadows must merge with the night. When you can smell the smoke, draw your weapons and advance up to the wall. The seiðmenn will attempt to flee or use their dark arts against us. Cut them down on sight.' Arinbjørn nodded and started to move to the left, but Eirik's hand still held him fast by the shoulder. 'And get your men out of there before anybody gets injured. You are responsible for them. Understood?'

Arinbjørn's chin dipped in a terse nod. 'Understood,' he replied, a barely audible whisper.

When Eirik let go of his shoulder, Arinbjørn sneaked forty paces back to the band of housecarls hiding under cover of the fir trees.

'Atle, pick six men and follow me,' he said in a low voice. Then, Arinbjørn himself pointed at five nearby warriors, one at a time.

Moments later, Arinbjørn crouched and stalked around the glade, followed by twelve of Eirik's housecarls. He had not seen any guards when he scouted the farm before sundown, but now and then, the door would open, and one or two men would leave the building to relieve themselves. For all he knew about sorcerers, they might have unseen spirits guarding them while they feasted. There were at least three doors in the main building, indicating it had been used to house livestock as well as people. He could not discount the possibility of other exits as well.

When he reached their position on the east side of the longhouse, Arinbjørn knelt, held up one arm and waved his hand in a circular motion. The twelve warriors gathered around him. He felt a surge of trepidation when he found Alv Ossutsson among the men Atle had picked. A pang of unease settled in Arinbjørn's chest. Gunnhild's brother now fell under his protection.

Arinbjørn pointed at two men carrying bows and then at two nearby trees ten paces apart. He thought while he waited for the archers to find their positions. It was dark now, but as soon as the building caught fire, it would be easy for the archers to find targets. Ideally, he would have preferred Alv to be one of them, but the boy had no aptitude for archery. Arinbjørn found an alternative and indicated for Alv to come closer.

'Draw your sword and cover the archers,' Arinbjørn whispered.

He heard Alv draw a breath, as if about to voice his thoughts, but then silence enveloped them both. Arinbjørn knew he would have to address Alv's disappointment later, but for now, their focus had to be on the task at hand.

With the palms of his hands downward, Arinbjørn signalled for the others to crouch. Then, he turned towards the longhouse and waited.

Based on the sounds, he tried to envision what had happened inside. Some noises were familiar, of the kind one usually heard at a feast. There were loud voices, shouting, laughter and pounding on tables. But there were also strange sounds, songs and chants that chilled him to the bone. They were up against fourscore sorcerers and who knows how many evil spirits.

Arinbjørn had fought by Eirik's side at the battle of the Dvina in Bjarmeland, where they routed the enemy and won a great victory. But that was in bright daylight, and the enemies were in plain sight.

The stinging scent of burning tar brought Arinbjørn back from the memories of his first battle, and he remembered Eirik's orders. Slowly, he drew his sword and held it aloft for the others to see. Staring intently at the menacing longhouse, he waited until the rustling behind him faded before he pointed ahead with the tip of his sword. He cowered to make himself as small as possible as he ran as silently as he could over the open field and found comfort in hearing his companions following suit. Thirty quick steps brought him to the wall, and he put his back to the timber while he waited for the others. He grimaced at every sound, imagining it might alert dozens of sorcerers of their presence.

The chanting thundered against the logs at his back. Arinbjørn could not discern the words, only feel their power. Then started the stomping of feet. The wall shook, and the ground trembled as the sorcerers jumped and danced inside. The noise grew ever higher, and the dancing was faster and more violent until one voice stood out from the others and tore through the chanting like a sword through a sail.

'Fire! Fire!' someone cried.

Arinbjørn tried to imagine the scene inside, that he might foresee their reactions. The eerie chanting and frenzied dancing abruptly ceased, giving way to a cacophony of shouts and frantic attempts to breach the fortified walls. The echo of an axe striking the logs reverberated through the air, its source somewhere to the left of Arinbjørn. Something slammed into the wall behind him and broke. A bench, or a table? Another axe was put to use. Arinbjørn could smell the wisps of smoke seeping out between the logs. Coughing. Screams of fear, of despair, of pain.

Everyone in the same building, with no sentries?

Arinbjørn promised himself to never put himself in that position.

Loud sounds of wood breaking were followed by intensified shouting and screaming. A wave of heat washed over Arinbjørn's back, and he stepped a few paces away from the wall. The sorcerers must have broken up the door or made a hole in the wall, providing more air for the all-consuming flames.

'Back up,' he ordered his companions. 'The fire ...'

His command was interrupted when somebody landed on his shoulder and brought him to the ground. Arinbjørn tensed in anticipation of an axe or a blade between his ribs, but nothing happened. He looked up and saw two men running towards the woods. Towards the archers, and the boy Alv. The queen's brother, who was under *his* protection.

He could only watch as the fleeing sorcerers ran straight at them. A bowstring sang, then another. One sorcerer fell, the other kept running. With dread, Arinbjørn saw Alv emerge from the trees, sword in hand. He charged at the oncoming enemy, but at the last moment crouched and swung his sword sideways against the sorcerer's knees. There was a loud sound of severed flesh and broken bones, followed by a wail. Alv got to his feet, closed the distance to his prone foe and thrust his sword into his back.

Arinbjørn snapped into action and rose.

'Back up, back up! They are jumping from the roof!'

Half a dozen men jumped—or fell—from the roof. Their clothes were on fire, and they almost seemed to welcome the deadly axe blows as relief. Then, flames broke through the roof, making it impossible to escape that way.

Arinbjørn's company moved further from the heat of the blazing building and listened in silence to the last screams from inside. The acrid stench of burning flesh assaulted their nostrils, causing Atle to empty the contents of his stomach on to the ground.

'Well done, Arinbjørn,' King Eirik said from behind him. 'Victory is ours!'

PART THREE

Rivals

CHAPTER: BJØRN FARMANN

Tønsberg, Viken, 927

The shadows cast long stretches as King Eirik sailed into Tønsberg harbour with three longships. A score of men, carrying shields and axes, gathered on the pier, their sombre mood barely stifling King Eirik's unwavering confidence. After two summers and one winter of successful raiding in Courland, his spirit soared, and his coffers overflowed.

'Where is my brother?' King Eirik bellowed, his voice echoing off the pier.

Silence met his query. Frustrated, Eirik opted for a more formal approach.

'King Eirik Haraldsson, heir to King Harald Fairhair, seeks an immediate audience with his brother, Bjørn Haraldsson Farmann!' Arinbjørn declared, his words resonating through the stillness.

Again, no reply.

'Bah!' Eirik erupted, leaping on to the pier before his crew could secure the ropes. Arinbjørn winced, observing his king's unsteady sea legs after a full day on the ship. Assured that Eirik wouldn't tumble back aboard, Arinbjørn followed suit, bracing himself, with young Alv Ossutsson trailing close behind.

'Where's my brother?' King Eirik repeated, his voice demanding answers. This time, he seized a nearby warrior, seemingly prepared to shake an answer out of him.

'Largest storehouse, up there,' the warrior stuttered, his fear evident. Most men cowered in the presence of the great Eirik Haraldsson.

Rather than releasing the man, Eirik gave him a forceful shove, causing him to stumble backwards and land on his rear. A few companions chuckled, though not nearly as loudly as Eirik's crew.

Arinbjørn approached the embarrassed warrior, extending a helping hand. 'Thank you. You've been most helpful.'

The man nodded, his grimace remaining stern.

With swift strides, Arinbjørn caught up with King Eirik and Alv as they entered a tall storage building. A young boy, scarcely twelve or thirteen winters, held the door open for them.

Contrary to expectations, the interior surpassed Arinbjørn's imaginings. Rather than a musty storehouse, they stepped into a tidy great hall, filled with the pleasant aromas of southern cuisine and exotic spices. Scored torches illuminated vibrant tapestries, gleaming weapons, and intricate metal, bone and woodwork. Upholstered chairs and benches lined the sides of massive, long tables, but an absence of a throne or high seat caught Arinbjørn's attention.

'Welcome, brother,' a youthful voice greeted them, devoid of fear or enthusiasm.

Arinbjørn turned to the right, finding a young man splendidly dressed in garments of linen and silk.

King Eirik burst into laughter. 'You look prettier than my wife!'

Bjørn Farmann offered a polite smile and nodded. 'Thank you, brother. Your words honour me.'

Eirik's tone shifted. 'That wasn't my intention. You dress like a woman, dishonouring yourself and our father, the king.

Why would you do that?'

Bjørn remained calm despite the insults. 'For the same reason you wear chain mail and wield an axe, I dress for the role I perform.'

Eirik's face soured. 'You still look like a woman.'

Unperturbed, Bjørn stared at his half-brother with a bored expression, refusing to dignify the comment with a response. Arinbjørn averted his gaze, knowing better than to insult their host.

'My men are hungry,' Eirik declared after an awkward pause, 'and thirst.'

'Of course.' Bjørn bowed deeply, another foreign custom. 'My steward has ensured there is ample food and drink for your men tonight. It will be my pleasure to hold a feast in your honour.'

Eirik laughed, clasping Bjørn's arm. 'There might be hope for you yet!'

At the feast, Bjørn arranged for a high seat to be raised for his older brother, while he occupied a more modest chair beside him. The large room resounded with songs and laughter as Eirik's men revelled in a rich selection of food and drink. Two other buildings served as feasting halls for those of King Eirik's men who could not be accommodated in the main hall. Dozens of house thralls and servants ensured the drinking horns remained filled until guests tumbled from their seats or dozed off at the table.

'I regret my harsh words when we first met, Bjørn,' King Eirik slurred, his speech muddled by ale. 'Despite my insults, you've been a gracious host to me and my men.'

Arinbjørn smiled, observing the potential for wisdom and politeness in Eirik Haraldsson, given enough time.

Bjørn lifted his drinking horn, saluting his brother. 'Thank you, Eirik. I'm glad our improvised feast has met your expectations.'

Eirik leaned closer, his voice lowering. 'You must visit me on Svanøy when you have the chance.'

'I will make sure to visit the next time I am in the vicinity,' Bjørn replied, a mischievous smirk playing on his lips.

Eirik cleared his throat, adopting a deeper tone. 'Come to think of it, I can offer you a favour right away.'

Bjørn cocked his head, raising an eyebrow. 'How?'

'I've come to collect your tribute on behalf of our father, the king.'

Bjørn Farmann's eyes narrowed. 'Is that so?'

'Yes,' Eirik persisted, undeterred by his brother's lack of enthusiasm. 'It's the least I can do. From what I've seen, you've been quite prosperous. Half of your revenue would be a precious shipment, sailing past Danes and Vikings eager to seize your treasure.'

'I'll take my chances,' Bjørn stated, his gaze fixed on his drinking horn.

'I must insist!' Eirik proclaimed. 'King Harald has named me his underking and heir to the throne.'

'Congratulations,' Bjørn muttered.

'With my title comes the right to collect taxes owed to the king of Norway,' Eirik pressed.

Bjørn Farmann drew a deep breath, exhaling slowly. 'I thank you for your generous offer, and I assure you the king of Norway will receive his taxes. But I will deliver them myself, as I always have.'

Eirik rose from his seat, looming over their young host. 'Must I remind you that I am your superior, with an army of seasoned warriors ready to enforce my decision?'

Bjørn turned, a smirk playing on his lips, as he observed King Eirik's renowned warriors, incapacitated in their drunken stupor.

'You mean those? I'll take my chances.'

For the first time that night, Arinbjørn noticed that many of those he believed were mere servants had long knives or axes strapped to their belts. Dozens of armed men had been present on the pier upon their arrival. King Eirik's indisposed army lay at their host's mercy.

Bjørn Farmann rose. 'Now, if you deem your men suitably fed, I suggest you seize the opportunity to return to your ships and depart. I've heard too many tales of scores of men trapped inside burning buildings after such a feast, and I would detest if that fate befell any of us.'

CHAPTER: ROLLO

Svanøy, Firdafylke

Gunnhild dabbed her middle finger in a vial of scented oil, applying it to her neck on both sides. She had spent the morning bathing, combing her hair, and donning her favourite dress. Although unremarkable in colour and fabric, it accentuated her curves perfectly. Eirik had certainly appreciated it the last time he saw her wearing it.

She let her hands glide along her sides and over her bottom, nodding in approval. Today marked the first time she wore it since the first months of her pregnancy. The snug fit would likely make it even more effective.

'How do I look, Astrid?' she asked, turning a full circle on the floor.

'You look gorgeous, my queen,' the maid replied.

'What else could you possibly say?' Gunnhild mumbled.

'What?' said Astrid.

'Nothing important,' Gunnhild dismissed. 'Would you please bring my son to me?'

'Of course, my queen,' Astrid replied and left the room.

Gunnhild shook her head, lightly tousling her hair to liven it up. Eirik preferred it loose. She smiled and slipped on her shoes.

Moments later, Astrid returned, carrying her baby boy in her arms. Gamle wasn't crying, but he wriggled and grunted, seemingly displeased with something.

'There you are!' Gunnhild exclaimed in her cheerful mother's voice. She reached out and lifted him from the maid's arms.

Gamle fell silent, staring at her with wide eyes. Shortly after, he squeezed his eyes shut and grimaced while flailing his short arms.

'Oh, stop it!' Gunnhild said. 'Let's go.'

She shifted Gamle in her arms, resting his back against her bosom as they walked. Gamle sobbed a few times, but his curiosity quieted as they made their way across the yard towards the great hall. Astrid hurried past them to open the door.

'Thank you, Astrid. Now, run down to the pier and inform the king that I'm waiting for him here.'

'Of course, my queen.'

As a wife, Gunnhild would have preferred to welcome her husband in their private chambers after a year apart, but that wasn't suitable for a king and queen. Therefore, she had asked their host, Tore Roaldsson, to prepare his great hall for their reception.

Gunnhild entered the hall and assumed her customary position for waiting on formal occasions. After a few heartbeats, a flustered young servant rushed to her side to announce her arrival.

'Queen Gunnhild,' he called.

The two men sitting at the innermost table rose to greet her.

'My queen,' Tore Roaldsson said with a polite nod. 'And Gamle Eiriksson,' he added, noticing the baby in her arms.

Gunnhild smiled and walked through the hall, savouring the scents of spiced meat and freshly baked bread. Tore Roaldsson's table was as impressive as ever, befitting a king's feast. She counted plates for two dozen guests.

'You are truly a generous host, Tore,' Gunnhild said with a smile, 'and a dear friend.'

Tore Roaldsson smiled and nodded in agreement.

'Hello, Øyvind,' Gunnhild greeted her brother. 'How kind of you to join us and celebrate my husband's return. Is King Fairhair treating you well at Avaldsnes?'

Øyvind looked down and cleared his throat. 'I've seen little of the king, and I'm not sure he knows I exist. But his hirdmen treat me well ... well enough, I suppose.'

'Do you train every day? Are you learning from them?'

Øyvind looked up. 'Yes, sister. I am growing stronger and more skilled with weapons each day,' he replied, his voice exuding newfound confidence.

'I'm pleased to hear that,' Gunnhild replied. 'You should be prepared to accompany my husband on his next voyage, wherever it may take you. I will discuss it with him.'

'Thank you, Gunnhild.' Øyvind beamed.

Gunnhild found her seat at the head of the table, in an ornate chair next to the king's high seat. Gamle immediately began to fuss, coughing and grunting. She resisted the temptation to hand him over to someone else. Gamle was her son and the heir to the throne after Eirik. It was the queen's duty to introduce him to his father.

'While we wait, would you care for something to eat?' Tore offered.

'No, thank you,' Gunnhild replied with a polite smile. 'But you might provide me with some news, particularly on matters the king should know. Eirik pays little attention to such affairs when he's raiding.'

Tore laughed. 'I suppose you're right, my queen. There isn't much you don't already know, but I recently heard some news from Francia.'

'Please, enlighten me,' Gunnhild said, rising and pacing

back and forth to soothe Gamle.

'Do you remember Rolv Ragnvaldsson?'

'No. Should I?'

'You probably know him as Gange-Rolv, son of Ragnvald Mørejarl.'

'Oh, the man who was supposedly too large to ride a horse? I never believed that story. Is he still alive?'

'Yes, he is, and he's nearly as old as King Harald. Fairhair outlawed him forty winters ago when he discovered that Rolv had been plundering in Viken.'

'As he should,' Gunnhild commented in a hushed voice, while Gamle continued to fuss and squirm in her arms.

'Well, Rolv carved out a realm for himself. He conquered Rouen, and the king of Francia named him Jarl of Normandy. He is now known as Rollo.'

'Oh, I have heard of Rollo of Normandy. I did not realise Rollo and Gange-Rolv were the same man. However, this hardly qualifies as news. Has he passed away?'

'No, not yet. But Rolv is an old man, weakened in mind and body. He has decided to step aside and pass his title and responsibilities to his son, Vilhelm.'

Gunnhild gazed at Tore in silence for a moment before responding, 'Thank you, Tore. That is an intriguing thought.'

CHAPTER: GAMLE

Moments later, Astrid slipped through the door and quick-stepped towards Gunnhild.

'My queen, King Eirik is on his way. He was right behind me.'

'Thank you, Astrid.'

Before anyone could utter another word, the door swung open.

'King Eirik!' the servant announced. After a brief pause, he added, 'Arinbjørn Toresson and Alv Ossutsson.'

Once again, Tore and Øyvind rose from their seats and turned towards the door.

Eirik entered, striding towards them, though his smile appeared forced. Gunnhild sensed an underlying unease. It seemed like a dark cloud loomed over him. She patiently waited for the men to exchange their customary banter and awkward hugs.

Gunnhild exchanged warm smiles with Arinbjørn and her brother, Alv. However, no one dared to interrupt the reunion of the king and queen.

'Gunnhild, my wife!' Eirik finally exclaimed. 'You look ...' He halted his words and movement when his eyes fell upon the baby in Gunnhild's arms.

'Welcome home, husband,' Gunnhild greeted. 'You didn't tell me how I look. Please, do continue,' she teased.

'Well, you look ... Is that one mine?' Eirik seemed flustered.

'Of course he is! Did you expect your queen to bear anyone else's child in your absence?'

'No, probably not. Is it a boy?' Eirik inquired.

'Yes,' Gunnhild beamed. 'Your firstborn son.'

Eirik furrowed his brow, a sign that he was deep in thought, before asking, 'How old is he?'

'Four months,' Gunnhild replied, maintaining her smile as she patiently waited for Eirik to make his calculations.

Eventually, Eirik nodded.

Gunnhild offered Gamle for his father to hold. Eirik accepted, cradling the infant in his strong, calloused hands. Father and son stared at each other in silence, their curiosity and insecurity intertwined.

'Does he have a name?' Eirik asked in a whisper.

'I named him Gamle,' Gunnhild responded.

Eirik grimaced. 'Gamle? That translates to old. How can a newborn be old?'

Gunnhild chuckled. 'He looked old. Wrinkled and grumpy.'

'He is the heir to the throne,' Eirik stated. 'I want to name him Harald, after my father.'

'Not this one,' Gunnhild said firmly.

Eirik's gaze narrowed. 'How do you know?'

Gunnhild met his stare head-on. 'How do I know anything?'

Eirik nodded and directed his attention back to his son, who was growing restless again. 'Well, maybe ...'

'He's less wrinkled now, but he's still temperamental most of the time. And he smells,' Gunnhild commented. 'Astrid, would you please take him back to our chambers, have him fed and bathed?'

'Of course, my queen.' Astrid promptly obeyed, taking the

baby with her.

Gunnhild and Eirik watched as the maid departed with their son.

'Besides, the king of Denmark is called Gamle,' Gunnhild offered.

'That's because he's old. His name is Gorm. People only started calling him Gamle in his later years,' Eirik argued.

'Well, I tried. You can name the next one,' Gunnhild said with a playful tone.

'Will there be another one?'

'I certainly hope so,' Gunnhild teased, flashing her most alluring smile. 'But I think we should attend to this feast first.'

CHAPTER: COUNCIL

The feast carried on. Gunnhild, Eirik, Tore and Arinbjørn found themselves seated at the head of the table, somewhat isolated from the rest of the guests. Alv and Øyvind, positioned below them, seemed more interested in mingling with the livelier company further down the table, leaving vacant spaces on either side.

Sensing an opportunity, Gunnhild decided to broach Eirik's worries before he became too intoxicated to hold a coherent conversation. She leaned in, her voice filled with genuine concern. 'Eirik, how was your journey?'

His response lacked enthusiasm. 'Profitable enough.'

Pressing further, Gunnhild inquired, 'Did we suffer many losses?'

Eirik's reply was curt. 'Some.'

Not one to be deterred, Gunnhild persisted, her voice tinged with a mixture of curiosity and worry. 'You appear troubled. What transpired during your travels?'

Eirik grimaced, downing the last remnants of his drink before answering, 'I made a stop at Bjørn Farmann's on our way back.'

'And?'

A trace of bitterness laced Eirik's words as he spoke. 'I offered to collect taxes on my father's behalf, as is my right. But Bjørn refused.'

Gunnhild's brow furrowed. She leaned closer, her voice gentle yet persistent. 'And then what?'

'Bjørn refused,' Eirik repeated, his tone laden with frustration as he took another sip from his empty horn.

A moment of silence passed between them. Gunnhild shifted her gaze to Tore, seeking additional insights. 'Tore, what can you tell me about Bjørn Farmann?'

Tore nodded. 'I only met him once when Bjørn was about Øyvind's age, sixteen or seventeen winters ago. He left quite an impression—a sharp, amiable young man. Over the years, he has made remarkable strides in business, establishing his dominance in Viken's trade. Lately, he has expanded his ventures into Denmark, Saxony and Friesland, with an impressive fleet of ships.'

Gunnhild's concern deepened, and she probed further. 'Do you think he poses a threat to Eirik?'

Tore's reply carried a note of reassurance. 'Bjørn is a merchant, not a warrior. He would never dare challenge King Eirik on the battlefield.'

Sensing there was more to the story, Gunnhild persisted. 'But ...?'

Tore's gaze turned sombre, his voice low. 'Bjørn has amassed wealth and loyalty. Although he may not aspire to be king himself, if he were to lend his resources to support his brother Olav in Viken, they would gain a considerable advantage.'

'What if Åsa's three sons in Trøndelag join forces with Olav and Bjørn?' Gunnhild pressed.

Tore winced, his expression betraying the gravity of the situation.

'That's enough!' Eirik declared, his voice filled with determination. 'We set sail for Tønsberg in two days' time. Tonight, we drink.'

CHAPTER: SEM

Tønsberg, Viken

It was well past midnight when two swift longships approached Tønsberg, one from the east and one from the west. King Eirik's ship sailed past the town, continuing towards Bjørn Farmann's estates at Sem, situated a short distance northwest of Tønsberg.

The other ship, captained by Arinbjørn, rowed into Tønsberg harbour from the east. A handful of warriors jumped on to the pier and disposed of a couple of confused guards before they managed to wake up their companions.

Keeping his voice low to avoid waking the town, Arinbjørn gave his commands. 'Three squads of ten. Take this building, that one, and that one. Eliminate anyone who poses a threat, seize whatever you can, and return to the ships before the townspeople take up arms.' Arinbjørn pointed to three storehouses in the harbour, including the one where they had recently feasted with Bjørn Farmann.

Arinbjørn kept a dozen men in reserve by the ship and stayed behind with them, listening to the scattered sounds of looting. An axe striking against a door, or an unfortunate witness; grunts and short cries from victims who met their fate moments after waking up; and shouting from confused townspeople trying to fathom what was happening down by the harbour—the latter growing more frequent as time passed.

Relieved to see the first of his crew returning with their plunder, Arinbjørn took a moment to observe their victorious, if not hasty, retreat. Drawing in a deep breath, he turned to Alv Ossutsson, who had just emerged from the large storehouse. 'Did you see Bjørn Farmann?'

Alv shook his head and spoke. 'No, but a servant revealed that Bjørn travelled to his estate at Sem before dusk.'

Arinbjørn glanced towards the northwest, searching for any signs of fires in the distance. 'King Eirik will soon arrive, and he may face staunch resistance from Bjørn's hird. We must hurry to support him.' He turned to his crew, raising his voice. 'Cast off! Man the oars! We're departing.'

As the ship gained speed, Arinbjørn took count of his crew and realised that one man was missing. 'Where is Onund?' he asked, concerned.

Atle, Berg-Onund's brother, replied, 'He was with us during the looting, but I lost sight of him in the storehouse.'

Arinbjørn pressed further. 'Did you hear any signs of a struggle?'

'Some, but nothing that indicated he was in danger,' Atle responded, his voice tinged with concern.

Arinbjørn looked back at Tønsberg, now fading in the distance to the east, its lights indicating that the townspeople had awoken and would soon discover what had transpired. If Berg-Onund was still alive, they might interrogate him.

His voice dropped to a murmur, almost lost in the splashes of the oars striking the water. 'Berg-Onund's fate is out of our hands.' Arinbjørn clenched his jaw, trying to push the knot of worry away. He glanced back towards Tønsberg one last time, then focused on the task at hand. 'Our king needs us. Continue on to Sem.'

Soon, their ship beached next to King Eirik's vessel at the shallow estuary below Sem. Similar to their actions in Tønsberg, Arinbjørn left a portion of his force to guard the ship, but this time he did not remain behind. Instead, he led his thirty warriors through the fields towards Bjørn Farmann's estate.

Arinbjørn could see at least a dozen sources of light ahead but heard no sounds of battle—only agitated voices.

Upon reaching the main buildings, Arinbjørn found King Eirik's warriors surrounding the estate, while Bjørn Farmann's men emerged to face them.

Bjørn stood tall with a torch in his left hand. His eyes locked with King Eirik's as he greeted him with a hint of bitterness in his voice. 'Welcome, brother!' he spoke, his tone devoid of any illusions about Eirik's true intentions. 'Have you come to share another feast with me?'

Eirik's reply was cold. 'No, Bjørn. I am your king, and I have come to claim what is rightfully mine.'

A wry smile played on Bjørn's lips as he retorted, his voice laced with defiance. 'By force, not right.'

Eirik's face tightened, his voice carrying a hint of steel. 'Your choice, not mine.'

Bjørn's eyes narrowed, his grip on his sword tightening. 'You may be a king, Eirik, but power is earned through the respect and loyalty of those who follow. Tell me, do your subjects truly stand behind you, or do they merely cower in fear?'

Eirik's jaw clenched. 'They stand behind me because they believe in the strength of our realm, a kingdom that will endure.'

Bjørn chuckled darkly. 'Is that what you tell yourself, Eirik? The truth is, you rule through fear and force, not through the loyalty and respect you claim. You sit on a throne of twigs, as old and brittle as our father.'

Eirik's hand tightened around the hilt of his sword, his voice dripping with disdain. 'You underestimate me, Bjørn. I have faced greater challenges than you can fathom, and I have always emerged victorious. Your defiance ends here.'

The tension between them hung heavy in the air, each word a hammer blow at any hope of reconciliation between the half-brothers. Bjørn, refusing to yield, drew his sword with a fluid motion, its blade glinting in the torchlight. 'You may end my defiance, Eirik Bloodaxe, but the people of Viken will always defy you.'

Sparks flew as sword and axe clashed, and the clash of steel filled the air. After the initial attacks, they began circling each other, their eyes locked in a battle of wills. When Eirik attacked again, it became clear that his experience and strength would be the deciding factor. Bjørn was driven back step by step.

With a final, decisive blow, Eirik's axe found its mark, slicing through Bjørn's defences and bringing him to his knees.

Bjørn, bloodied and weakened, gazed up at Eirik with a mix of defiance and resignation. 'You may have won this day, Eirik, but remember this: true power is not measured solely in might.'

With a swift and decisive strike, Eirik's axe found its mark, and Bjørn fell to the ground, his defiant spirit extinguished.

Arinbjørn felt a pang of sorrow for Bjørn. Despite their different paths, the young merchant had won his respect with his wisdom, his manners and his worldly knowledge. Under another sky, in another life, they could have been friends.

The remaining defenders, witnessing their leader's defeat, found themselves surrounded and outnumbered. They fought valiantly, but the outcome was inevitable. One by one, they met their demise at the hands of Eirik's warriors, their resistance snuffed out in the face of overwhelming force.

'Ransack this place!' King Eirik commanded. 'Take everything of value. But return to the ships before first light, or we will leave without you! The people of Tønsberg will soon tire of our presence.'

The remark made Arinbjørn think of Berg-Onund, who was left behind with the enraged townspeople in Tønsberg. He decided to refrain from plundering, and rather go search for his friend. As he turned to leave, he collided with someone standing right behind him.

'At least the king warns his men before he leaves them

behind.'

'Berg-Onund!' Arinbjørn's voice was a mix of relief and disbelief. 'How did you get here?'

Berg-Onund, still panting from the exertion, managed a weak smile. 'I ran.'

Despite the tension, Arinbjørn couldn't help but laugh, the relief overwhelming the grim circumstances, if only for a moment.'

'I was just on my way to go look for you.'

Berg-Onund smiled. 'I know you were.'

CHAPTER: ADVISER

Selva, Trøndelag

Herlaug Håvardsson could not contain his enthusiasm as he shared a piece of local history with King Eirik. 'Did you know, King Eirik, that Grjotgard Herlaugsson, my grandfather, once resided here on Selva?'

Eirik, not particularly attentive to their talkative host, responded with a lack of enthusiasm. 'Who?'

Herlaug chuckled, slightly surprised. 'But you jest! Of course, you know my grandfather, the great Grjotgard Herlaugsson of Håløygaland. He was the father of Jarl Håkon Grjotgardsson of Lade, your father's ally!'

Eirik's face lit up with a spark of recognition. 'Ah, yes. I recall now. He was killed by a berserk if I'm not mistaken.'

'Indeed!' Herlaug affirmed, pride lacing his voice. 'Right here on Selva!'

Arinbjørn breathed a silent sigh of relief. The night had seen King Eirik consume countless horns of ale, and it wouldn't have been the first time he insulted a host in his drunken state, whether out of ignorance or arrogance.

Curiosity apparently getting the better of him, Eirik inquired, 'How did you come to inherit this farm, Herlaug?'

Herlaug beamed with pride as he explained, 'My father was Håvard, the youngest son of Grjotgard, and the brother of Håkon and Sigurd. When Grjotgard father fell in battle, Håkon became the jarl of Lade, and Sigurd returned to Sandnes in Håløygaland. Selva passed to my father, and I later inherited it from him.'

'And you remain loyal to King Harald and his kin?' Eirik probed.

'Of course! The alliance between our families has always been strong, reinforced through several marriages,' Herlaug responded.

Arinbjørn nodded in understanding. King Harald Fairhair had employed such strategies to solidify his power. However, Eirik showed little interest in such matters.

'I'm pleased to hear that,' Eirik acknowledged. 'I'm on my way to Lade for negotiations with your cousin, Jarl Sigurd Håkonsson.'

'Really? On what occasion?' Herlaug inquired.

Arinbjørn, aware of the sensitive nature of political discussions, knocked his ale horn forcefully against the table, attempting to capture Eirik's attention and steer him away from engaging in such matters with a farmer from Trøndelag. Unfortunately, his efforts were in vain, as Eirik started replying to Herlaug's question.

'King Eirik,' Arinbjørn interjected, 'a word, please?'

Eirik shot him an angry glance. 'Not now, Arinbjørn. Can't you see I'm in conversation with our host?'

'I do see that, my king. But I have received urgent news from the queen,' Arinbjørn insisted.

Eirik looked around the hall. 'She has sent a messenger? Where is he? Why did he not come to me directly?'

'Join me outside, and I will explain,' Arinbjørn proposed, hoping to defuse Eirik's anger.

Reluctantly, Eirik rose from his seat and followed Arinbjørn out the door.

Once outside, Arinbjørn grabbed a handful of fresh snow and rubbed it on his face, hoping to clear his mind and buy some time. He briefly entertained the idea of doing the same to the king but thought better of it as he observed the fierce expression on Eirik's face.

'What is it?' Eirik demanded impatiently.

Arinbjørn took a deep breath, choosing his words carefully. 'I need to piss first,' he replied, using the excuse to delay the conversation and allow Eirik to cool down.

'I suppose ...,' Eirik reluctantly conceded.

Once finished, Eirik grew more insistent. 'Where is the messenger?'

'I am the messenger,' Arinbjørn said.

Eirik shook his head in disbelief. 'And what is your message, Arinbjørn?'

Arinbjørn took another deep breath, knowing the news he was about to deliver would have a profound impact. 'The queen'—he hesitated for effect—'is with child.'

It was not a lie. Gunnhild's pregnancy had been evident to all during their last visit home.

Eirik's brows knitted together, his lips twisting into a snarl of incredulity. 'And you interrupted my conversation with our host to tell me this?'

'No, I interrupted *because* of your conversation with our host,' Arinbjørn clarified, hoping to make Eirik understand the gravity of the situation.

Eirik's face contorted with confusion.

'We are in Trøndelag, my king,' Arinbjørn explained. 'This is a hostile region!'

'Why? My father spent many winters here, and we are allied with the jarl of Lade,' Eirik argued.

'Sixty winters have passed since your father's time. After the slaying of Bjørn Farmann, your people do not hold the same affection for you,' Arinbjørn explained.

'Olav Haraldsson may have stirred up the people in Viken against me, but his rebellion means nothing to the people of

Trøndelag,' Eirik dismissed.

Arinbjørn revealed his deep knowledge of the region. 'Olav has held a council with your brothers in Trøndelag, Sigrød and Halvdan the Black.'

Eirik's eyes widened in surprise. 'How do you know?'

Arinbjørn's voice carried a hint of pride. 'How do I know anything? I have familiarised myself with your father's extensive network of informants. As your adviser, it is my duty to know such things.'

Eirik's expression turned sour. 'And what is your advice now?'

Arinbjørn's words were measured. 'Stop discussing matters of state with farmers.'

'Very well,' Eirik begrudgingly conceded.

'And stop drinking,' Arinbjørn added firmly.

'Why?' Eirik questioned, slightly taken aback.

'Because you are the king, and you need to stay alert when you are away from home,' Arinbjørn reminded him.

Eirik spat on the ground. 'Anything else?'

'Yes. Tonight, we will sleep in the small guesthouse—you, me, Berg-Onund, Alv and Øyvind. I have made the necessary arrangements. The rest of your hird will sleep in the longhouse,' Arinbjørn instructed.

Eirik questioned the decision. 'Why?'

'Because of Ragnvald and Bjørn, and many before them,' Arinbjørn said, his voice dropping to an ominous whisper. 'It seems to be unhealthy for sons of Fairhair to sleep in large buildings.'

Eirik protested, 'I have thirty men!'

Arinbjørn's voice grew serious. 'And how many do your brothers have?'

Eirik stared at Arinbjørn in silence for a moment before

finally nodding his head in reluctant agreement.

CHAPTER: ARSON

Arinbjørn sat up abruptly in bed, his heart pounding in his chest. A sense of unease washed over him, but he could not quite pinpoint the cause. Had it been a sound? Or perhaps just a dream? He strained his ears, but all he could hear was the soft snoring of King Eirik and his own rapid breathing. The feast must have come to an end, as there were no more songs or boisterous laughter resonating through the hall. The room was engulfed in darkness, with only fading embers in the fireplace providing a faint glow.

It was *ótta*—the darkest time of the night. Arinbjørn felt a chill run down his spine as he realised that something was amiss. He got out of bed, slipped on his shoes, and made his way to the door. Pushing it open slightly, he paused, his senses heightened. The silence was eerie, but not complete. It was the kind of silence that he had come to associate with people trying to move unnoticed. Faint sounds reached his ears—the muffled crunch of snow under heavy boots, barely audible whispers, and short, hushed commands.

Arinbjørn shut the door quietly and hurried to wake Berg-Onund, shaking his shoulder gently. Before Berg-Onund could speak, Arinbjørn placed a finger to his lips and whispered urgently, 'We are under attack. Wake the boys and get dressed.'

Turning his attention to King Eirik, Arinbjørn repeated the process. However, the king remained unresponsive, lost in a deep slumber. Frustration welled up within Arinbjørn as he received only a few grunts in response to his efforts. Determined to rouse the king, he leaned in closer and whispered directly into Eirik's ear, 'Eirik, wake up. They are coming for us. We must fight.'

Eirik stirred, his eyes fluttering open as he faced Arinbjørn. Arinbjørn's heart raced with relief at the sight of Eirik's awakening.

'Don't say a word,' Arinbjørn warned, his voice barely audible. 'Put on your shoes. We must leave before they find us.'

When his four companions stood on their feet, Arinbjørn quickly tied his shoes, secured his sword, and fastened his belt around his waist. He returned to the door, peeking outside. In the dim light, he spotted figures advancing towards the longhouse, approximately forty paces from the guesthouse where he had insisted Eirik be lodged during their stay at Selva. Torches illuminated the scene, revealing armed men pressed against the walls. Two individuals carried a barrel and a keg, while someone lay motionless near the entrance.

Arinbjørn contemplated waking the hirdmen in the longhouse but ultimately dismissed the idea. Instead, he closed the door and turned to face the others, his voice urgent yet steady. 'We are under attack, and we are outnumbered. The enemies have surrounded the longhouse, and it seems their intention is to set it ablaze.'

Eirik tightened his grip on his axe and started to move towards the door, but Arinbjørn halted him with a firm hand on his chest. 'Stop,' he whispered with intensity. 'You will be struck down before you can even reach the longhouse. They are here for you.'

'Let them have me,' Eirik growled, though he maintained the restraint of not raising his voice.

'No,' Arinbjørn asserted firmly. 'You are the king. We cannot win this battle. If you fall, everything falls. This time, you must flee.'

Eirik's eyes blazed with rage, his body trembling, but he managed to keep his voice controlled. 'And leave my men to burn?'

Arinbjørn's voice softened. 'The hirdmen have sworn to protect the king with their lives. The king must live and rule. Now, do your part.'

Reluctantly, Eirik turned to pick up his weapon shirt, but Arinbjørn quickly grasped his shoulder, halting him once again. 'There is no time. We must leave, now.'

Taking a deep breath, Arinbjørn opened the door just enough to slip out, wincing at the sound of the snow crunching beneath his feet. He waited for a few heartbeats, his senses on high alert, before taking the next step. He moved to the left, allowing the others to exit the guesthouse. With his back pressed against the wall, he pondered their escape plan.

The Agdenes headland extended northward, which meant any attacking force would approach from the south and east. If they followed the nearby river northeast, they would soon reach the sea—a small bay at the outer part of the long Trondheim fjord leading to Lade and beyond. Perhaps they could find a boat they could row, but where would they go? Would Jarl Sigurd Håkonsson of Lade offer them refuge? Or was he the mastermind behind this audacious attack on King Eirik?

The closest ally they could rely on was Jarl Tore Teiande of Giske. He was the son of Ragnvald Mørejarl and married to Ålov, Harald Fairhair's daughter. However, Giske lay far to the south, halfway between Selva and Svanøy. They could not hope to reach it solely by rowing. Fleeing northward would eventually lead them to the tip of the promontory, where they would have nowhere to run or hide.

A loud noise broke the stillness, drawing Arinbjørn's attention back to the longhouse. As he watched, the first flames licked up the wall. A similar sound followed, and there was another fire at the far end of the building. The assailants seemed determined to reduce Selva to ashes.

Arinbjørn made a swift decision and took charge. 'Follow

me,' he said firmly, leading the group down to the river. With each step, he could not help but notice the distinct imprints their feet made in the fresh snow. It was a trail that even a child could follow, making it clear that they could not risk fleeing over land.

Just then, the snap of a twig echoed from the woods behind them. All five of them instantly crouched, eyes meeting in a silent understanding. Eirik gestured toward a rocky outcrop to their right, and without a word, they moved.

They had barely concealed themselves behind the rocks when four armed men emerged from the forest, axe blades glinting ominously in the light from a single torch. A burly man with a vicious scar across his cheek, sniffed the air as if smelling their fear.

'I saw somebody try to escape this way. Search the area,' he growled.

Arinbjørn caught Eirik's eye and subtly gestured toward a loose rock at his feet. Understanding flashed between them. Eirik picked up the rock and, with a deep breath, hurled it into the woods to their left.

A startled bird took flight, drawing the enemies' attention. 'What was that? Go check it out,' the leader barked.

As the men dashed off into the woods, Arinbjørn and the others took their chance. Slipping away from their hiding place, they quickly descended towards the river, putting as much distance as they could between themselves and their foes.

'We're leaving tracks,' Alv said.

'That can't be helped, unless we learn to fly,' Arinbjørn replied.

Upon reaching the river, Arinbjørn guided them to the water's edge, where the snow had been washed away. The river had not yet frozen, as only two days had passed since the first snowfall. Crouching down, they followed the course of the river north-eastward, the icy water rising up to their knees. In the distance, the screams of the hirdmen rang through the night, blending with the glow of growing fires reflected in the river.

Arinbjørn raised his hand, signalling the group to stop as the river made a right turn. He pointed to Alv and Berg-Onund, then directed their attention to a copse of trees located south of the river, roughly fifty paces downstream. Without uttering a word, the two men drew their weapons and silently crossed the river. Arinbjørn crouched even lower, feeling the water brush against his back and soak his linen serk. Eirik and Øyvind followed suit, mimicking Arinbjørn's stealthy movements.

In the darkness, they peered towards the copse of trees, straining to discern any signs of movement. Something had stirred among the shadows, but the number or identity of the figures remained elusive. From behind, they could still hear the echoes of screams, shouts, and a disturbing laughter. Arinbjørn could not fathom what kind of vile creature would find amusement in the demise of so many men, but the answer would soon reveal itself.

Suddenly, a muffled cry from the south bank interrupted their thoughts and diverted Arinbjørn's attention from the dying hirdmen in the engulfed longhouse.

'THEY A—,' a man's voice shouted, but his words were abruptly cut off.

Moments later, Alv and Berg-Onund returned to the riverbank through the same path they had taken before. Alv had slung a shield over his back, concealing it from view.

Over the rushing sound of the river, Alv whispered, barely audible to the others, 'Two men. They will not reveal our presence.'

'Who is responsible for this?' Eirik whispered urgently, his voice laced with a mix of concern and determination.

Arinbjørn's gaze shifted to the shield hanging on Alv's back, its colours and patterns barely distinguishable in the dim light. The round shield featured a division into four equal parts

—two red and two black quarters.

'This shield bears the colours of Halvdan the Black,' Arinbjørn answered solemnly, the weight of the situation settling upon them all.

'Halvdan the Black?' Eirik's brows furrowed, his eyes narrowing with anger. 'What can he possibly gain from attacking us?'

Arinbjørn sighed, the gravity of the situation heavy in his voice. 'Halvdan seeks to challenge your rule, and this attack will serve as a warning to all who oppose him.'

Eirik clenched his fists, his jaw set in determination. 'He shall not go unpunished for this betrayal.'

Arinbjørn nodded, his eyes fixed the flickering glow of the distant fires. 'We must be cautious, my king. Halvdan has allies and supporters in Trøndelag. Our path forward will be treacherous.'

Eirik's gaze hardened, his voice filled with resolve. 'Halvdan will regret this day.'

Arinbjørn nodded. 'But first, we must ensure our survival. Let us find a way out of here.'

They followed the meandering path of the river, its icy waters flowing swiftly beneath them. The sound of rushing water filled their ears as they navigated through the left turn, drawing closer to the awaiting shore. Ahead of them, a cluster of sturdy boathouses formed a semicircle around the bay, their structures illuminated by the dim moonlight.

Eirik cast a swift glance at his longship and shook his head. 'Spread out and find a boat suitable for the five of us,' he commanded.

The group quickly set about their task, scanning the boathouses for a vessel that could accommodate their small party. Among the varied sizes and designs, they stumbled upon a sturdy *færing*, its weathered wood displaying the marks of many journeys. With a concerted effort, they half-lifted and half-dragged the boat into the water, readying it for their escape.

Berg-Onund took his position at the rear and pushed off. Alv's and Arinbjørn's hands gripped the oars with practised ease, their muscles tensing as they propelled the boat forward. The water churned beneath them as they embarked on their uncertain voyage, leaving behind the burning remnants of Selva and the echoes of destruction.

Arinbjørn lifted his gaze to face the shore they were leaving behind. The glow of flames cast an eerie light, revealing the smaller fires erupting around the burning longhouse. It was a devastating sight.

With their boat gliding through the water, Eirik broke the silence. 'Where shall we head now? Before this night, I would have said Lade, but now I'm reluctant to travel to the heart of Trøndelag.'

Arinbjørn turned his attention to Eirik, asking, 'How far is it from here to Giske?'

Eirik pondered for a moment. 'A short day of sailing with the longship, but we must row for two long days, even if the gods are kind to us.'

'They rarely are,' Arinbjørn replied. 'What about Hitra? It's within reach if we take turns with the oars. We can travel north around the promontory, then west along the coast. We should arrive by midday and hopefully find a ship willing to take us south.'

Eirik contemplated the suggestion. Finally, he nodded. 'Let it be so. We shall make our way to Hitra and seek support there.'

With their destination decided, they rowed away from the burning Selva.

CHAPTER: RETRIBUTION

Utstein, Rogaland

'I shall have his head for this!' King Harald Fairhair exclaimed, his pale skin flushed with anger as Eirik recounted his harrowing escape from Halvdan the Black.

The ageing king attempted to rise from his throne but faltered halfway, sinking back down. Strands of thin, white hair revealed patches of his scalp, and an unpleasant scent hung in the stale air of the small audience chamber at King Harald's winter quarters in Utstein.

Gunnhild, heavily pregnant, kept her distance, attributing her queasiness to her condition.

'I lost my hird in the fire,' Eirik stated, his voice filled with a mix of frustration and despair. 'Many others have returned to their homes for the winter. I haven't enough men to launch an attack on Halvdan in Trøndelag.'

'You don't, but I do!' Harald declared, his voice resolute.

Eirik drew a breath, seemingly about to speak, but remained silent.

King Harald turned his gaze from Eirik to Gunnhild, who looked down, avoiding eye contact.

'I shall lead my army to Lade and seek support from Håkon Jarl,' Harald declared confidently.

'Sigurd,' Eirik interjected, his voice barely above a whisper.

'What?' Harald responded, momentarily taken aback.

'Sigurd,' Eirik repeated. 'Håkon Jarl passed away many winters ago. His son, Sigurd, now holds the title of Jarl of Lade.'

A brief pause ensued, lasting no longer than three heartbeats. 'Yes, of course! I know the Jarl of Lade, just as I knew his father,' Harald acknowledged.

Eirik nodded, his eyes lowered.

Harald clapped his hands, summoning his steward. 'Kjartan!'

Within moments, the king's steward, Kjartan, appeared at his side. 'Yes, my king?'

'Summon Hauk. I need to discuss this campaign with him,' King Harald commanded.

Kjartan cleared his throat. 'My king, Hauk Håbrok is still in England with Haakon.'

'Is that so?' Harald's voice quivered, his hand trembling.

'Yes, my king,' Kjartan confirmed.

Gunnhild could not help admiring the steward's patience.

'Is there anyone else I can consult, someone who is familiar with the state of my army?' Harald asked, his voice filled with a mixture of desperation and uncertainty.

'My king, Kjetil Hundolfsson is now the leader of your hird. However, you granted him leave to spend Jól with his family in Sogn,' Kjartan replied.

'Yes ...' Harald seemed lost in thought.

'But perhaps you would like to speak with Guttorm Skald? He has recently returned from his travels and possesses valuable knowledge about recent events in your realm,' Kjartan suggested.

'Yes,' Harald agreed. 'Guttorm. Find him for me.'

'Of course, my king.' Kjartan bowed and hurried out of the room.

An uneasy tension settled in the audience chamber as they awaited the arrival of the skald. King Harald broke the silence.

'When is your baby due?' Harald inquired, catching Gunnhild off guard with his directness.

'My king,' she replied, taken aback, 'we shall welcome our son or daughter in the spring.'

'Good!' Harald exclaimed. 'You're halfway there, then. And how is your firstborn?'

'Gamle is hungry and healthy, my king. Thank you for asking,' Gunnhild responded, smiling warmly at the ageing king, her father-in-law.

A knock at the door interrupted their light conversation.

'My king,' Kjartan announced, 'Guttorm Sindre has arrived.'

'Ah, Guttorm! Thank you for joining us on such short notice,' Harald greeted him.

'My king,' Guttorm began, 'please forgive my dishevelled appearance. I would not have worn my travel attire had I known I was to have an audience with the king. But Kjartan insisted it was urgent.'

Gunnhild smirked, noting the immaculate attire of the skald. Tall leather boots, black wadmal trousers, a red linen shirt, and an exquisite dark blue cloak adorned with rings and necklaces—Guttorm's outfit was clearly meant to make a lasting impression, not for travel.

'It will suffice,' King Harald declared. 'You have recently returned from Viken. What news have you gathered?'

Guttorm licked his lips and glanced briefly at Eirik before speaking. 'Well, I'm afraid the ... elimination ... of Bjørn Farmann has made quite an impression on the people of Viken. They perceive Eirik Haraldsson as a threat, my king.'

'And?' Harald prompted.

'Furthermore, your son Olav has taken to calling himself the King of Viken,' Guttorm disclosed.

'We were aware of this,' Harald acknowledged. 'What else?'

'There is an alliance forming between Viken and Trøndelag. Olav has held two meetings with Sigrød and Halvdan the Black since ... since Bjørn Farmann's demise.'

'And the other Halvdan? The White?' Harald asked.

'Father,' Eirik replied, looking down and barely concealing a sigh, 'Halvdan the White perished while raiding in the east last summer.'

'Yes, yes, of course,' Harald recalled.

'Rumours also circulate about a potential alliance with the Danes,' Guttorm revealed.

'Why?' Eirik questioned. 'I have no quarrel with the Danes!'

'Without a strong Norwegian king, the Danes see an opportunity to resume pillaging our southern coast,' Harald explained. 'That's why many Danish kings and jarls fought against me at Hafrsfjord.'

Guttorm respectfully bowed in acknowledgement of the king's statement.

'Is there anything else?' Harald inquired.

'No, my king,' Guttorm replied. 'However, Viken and Trøndelag are preparing to fight for their independence. While they acknowledge your rule, they are unlikely to submit to Eirik when his time comes.'

'Very well,' Harald declared. 'We shall strike first, then.'

The king turned to Kjartan. 'Summon Kjetil Hundolfsson and the rest of my army. We will crush this rebellion before it gains further strength.'

Once again, Kjartan bowed and left the room.

'My king, if I might?' Guttorm interjected.

'Yes, skald?' Harald invited.

'I do not wish to overstep my bounds in matters of state and politics,' Guttorm began, his voice laced with concern. 'Yet, I am consumed by the deep-seated fear of the grave repercussions another kinslaying will bring upon us. Eirik's once noble reputation is now tarnished; he is known as Bloodaxe in Viken. The relentless execution of all those who dare oppose you will only sow seeds of discord, hindering the path towards a prosperous Norway. I implore you, for the sake of our beloved country and its people, to break this harrowing cycle of kinslaying that has plagued our land for far too long.'

Before Harald could respond, Gunnhild's voice cut through the air, brimming with urgency and desperation. 'My king! Halvdan the Black has unleashed the flames of war upon us. To allow him to live and fight another day, when the fires of rebellion have intensified, will surely plunge us deeper into the abyss. We must act swiftly to prevent further catastrophe!'

Harald's expression softened, revealing the weight of the burden he carried. 'Yes, Gunnhild, we're at war,' he confessed, his voice tinged with a mix of resignation and determination. 'But I shall nevertheless heed Guttorm's plea and carefully consider our course of action during my journey to Trøndelag. Our decisions in these troubling times must be made with utmost prudence and wisdom.'

CHAPTER:
SETTLEMENT

Utstein, Rogaland

'My queen,' Astrid said. 'King Fairhair returns with his fleet.'

Two moons had passed since the old king took his army to Trøndelag to punish Halvdan the Black for his treason. Gunnhild and Eirik spent the Jól at Utstein. They had received no messages regarding the outcome of the battle between Harald Fairhair and his wayward son, and Gunnhild suspected that was not a good sign.

'Thank you, Astrid.' Gunnhild rose from her bed, her face etched with discomfort. She had felt unwell the last fortnight, and a persistent ache gnawed at her. 'I don't think I shall brave the walk to the ships. But aid me with my attire and hair; I must present myself before King Harald shortly.'

Gunnhild tried three dresses before she decided on the first. They were just about done when Eirik entered without knocking.

'Eirik, you know better! A knock should precede your entry into a woman's quarters.' Gunnhild's voice held an edge of steel. Though not one to shy from a challenge, she felt herself not as formidable of late.

Eirik looked confused. 'I'm sorry. It never bothered you before.'

'It didn't.' Gunnhild sighed. 'Two more moons. Please, be patient with me.'

Eirik smiled and hugged her. 'Of course. But my father has summoned me to his chambers, and I thought you would want to join me.'

'Thank you. You are right, and I'm ready. Just let me hold your arm as we cross the yard.'

'Always!' Eirik said and held out his arm for her.

'Not now!' Gunnhild chided and slapped his arm.

After a slow and careful walk on the slippery ground, Gunnhild and Eirik entered King Harald's audience chambers. Harald was already there, half-asleep in his upholstered chair.

'My king,' Kjartan's voice rang out, 'your son stands ready.'

Gunnhild darted a pointed look at the steward.

'And Gunnhild,' he corrected hastily.

'Thank you, Kjartan,' King Harald said. 'Leave us, please.'

Kjartan bowed and left the room.

'Eirik,' Harald said, rising from his chair with considerable effort, 'and Gunnhild.'

King Harald Fairhair swayed and clutched the edge of the table to steady himself.

'Thank you for coming.' Harald said. 'Please, sit with me.'

Without a word, Eirik and Gunnhild sat next to the ageing king.

'Halvdan the Black will not challenge your claim to the throne, Eirik.'

'So, you won the battle?' Eirik said.

Harald shook his head slowly, his eyes downcast. 'No. There was no battle.'

'But ...'

'I brought my army to Halvdan and met with him. He promised he would not oppose you again.'

'You let him slip away,' Gunnhild remarked.

'You are harsh, my daughter,' Harald said, looking more sad than angered. 'But I cannot blame you, for I used to reason just like you do.'

King Harald seemed to study Gunnhild for some time. Or rather, his vacant stare was locked on her while he pondered what to say. He turned to Eirik.

'I'm spent, my son. There is no strength left in me. My body fails me. My mind fails me.'

'Don't speak like that!' Eirik said. 'You ...' He stopped talking when Gunnhild lay her hand on his arm.

'I'm no longer fit to rule, Eirik,' Harald said. 'I shall step aside and spend what remains of my life at Avaldsnes.'

Eirik merely nodded.

'I had hoped to fall in battle, but such an honourable end seems beyond me now. Perhaps this is for the best, for anyone who would best King Harald Fairhair in battle would likely claim the throne for himself.'

'Nobody could best you in battle, Father!' Eirik said.

'So it seemed for half a century. But age is an enemy beyond my powers.'

'I'm sorry,' Eirik said.

Gunnhild kept silent. This was a moment between father and son.

'Don't be. I have ruled longer than most men live. But now is your time, Eirik. In a fortnight, you shall be named King of Norway in the presence of jarls and hersirs. My estates, my lands, my army, my fleet, my wealth, my taxes, my rights and my responsibilities are all yours, King Eirik Haraldsson of Norway!'

Eirik rose and hugged his father.

Gunnhild felt relieved. It was the right decision, but still not an easy one.

'Now, leave me. I must plan the ceremony with Kjartan and Kjetil. Everything must be just right, so nobody can question your rightful claim to the throne.'

'Thank you, Father,' Eirik said, taking Gunnhild by the arm.

Just before they reached the door, she stopped and turned to King Harald.

'My king?' Gunnhild said.

'Yes, Gunnhild?' Harald said.

'I'm expecting a boy soon.'

Harald smiled. 'You know it is a boy?'

'Yes,' Gunnhild said. 'I want to name him Harald, if you don't object to sharing your name with your grandson.'

Harald's smile broadened. He cast a glance at Eirik, who confirmed with a short nod.

'Thank you for showing an old man such an honour,' King Harald said.

PART FOUR

Bloodaxe

CHAPTER: HALVDAN THE BLACK

Trøndelag, 932

Crouching low, Alv beckoned with an upturned palm. Gunnhild and Øyvind stilled, pressing their bodies against the pit house wall. Risking exposure, Alv stole a glance over the thatch.

'There is an unguarded door on the eastern wall of the longhouse,' Alv whispered.

Gunnhild tilted her face skyward, towards the moon. Sudden mirth roared from Sigrød Haraldsson's great hall.

'Too early,' she decreed. 'We bide our time.'

'Waiting for what?' Øyvind asked.

'Waiting for the mead to muddle their minds, too sotted to spot their queen serving their ale,' Gunnhild responded.

'You're courting trouble, sister,' Alv murmured, settling next to her. 'Dire consequences await if they catch you.'

'I face no greater danger than any warrior in my husband's hird.'

'But you are the queen,' Alv argued in hushed tones.

'I was not always a queen. I've learnt to outlive the cruel hand of fate and the depravity of men. With four sons of mine walking, should I meet my end this night, the kingdom will stand.'

Alv rose again, his gaze seeking the path above the low

thatch. 'What if they catch you tonight, Gunnhild? Sigrød and Halvdan could force Eirik's hand. They might demand he relinquish his claim on Trøndelag in exchange for your safe return.'

Gunnhild met his gaze with a chilling smile. 'That's why you are here with me, dear brother. To ensure that I do not survive to thrust our king into such a dilemma.'

Alv's eyes widened, his voice a strained whisper. 'We can't take on four dozen warriors to protect you. We're but two against many.'

'You misunderstand, Alv,' Gunnhild corrected, her voice unnervingly calm. 'You won't have to fight dozens of warriors. You'll have but one target—me.'

Alv recoiled, the shock making his voice too loud in the still night. 'You never breathed a word of this!'

Gunnhild winced. She glanced sideways at Øyvind, keeping watch to the right. He met her gaze in the dim light, shaking his head subtly in a silent plea for calm.

'Hush now, Alv,' Gunnhild warned, her voice a barely audible whisper. 'Quiet down, lest we all meet an untimely end tonight.'

'You misled us, Gunnhild,' Alv accused. 'You lured us with the promise of visiting our father.'

'And have I not fulfilled that promise?' Gunnhild shot back.

'Aye ... but you neglected to inform us of our detour to silence a rebel king in Trøndelag,' Alv argued, the frustration clear in his tone.

Gunnhild locked eyes with Alv, her question cold and hard. 'Had I told you the full plan, would you have joined me?'

Alv faltered. 'Aye, but ...'

Gunnhild leaned back against the rough wall of the pit house, her gaze steady on Alv, waiting for him to complete his thought. But words failed him, leaving them in an uncomfortable silence.

*

Under the pale light of a waning moon, Gunnhild discarded her traveller's cloak. Underneath, she was clad in the muted grey and brown attire of a serving girl. Though snug across her chest, such a fit was hardly a hindrance on a night like this. With a soft shake, she checked the small flask she had prepared, removing the cloth cap and slipping it into the secret pouch stitched into her shirt sleeve.

'The time is now,' she stated, her voice a whisper on the wind. 'If I fall into their clutches, you, Øyvind will return to Eirik with news of my demise, while, you, Alv stay behind to see it fulfilled.'

Their worried glances did not falter, yet they held their tongues as she walked away, towards the heart of Sigrød Haraldsson's great hall.

Gunnhild was a mere five strides from the door when it burst open. A man staggered out, stumbling forward in a desperate race with gravity. His race ended on his knees, emptying his stomach on the cold ground.

Seizing the moment, Gunnhild knelt beside the inebriated hirdman, waiting out his retching.

'Come now,' she coaxed, 'let's get you inside and rinse that taste away.'

He peered at her through bleary eyes, nodding in slow agreement.

'Good,' she replied, pulling him up.

Around her age, he had a broad frame and fair features that might've appealed under different circumstances. Steadying him, she guided him back into the warmth of the longhouse.

Inside, the hall of Sigrød was a grand spectacle. The

towering ceiling, upheld by robust beams adorned with painted carvings, dwarfed all below. The air was thick with the mingling of woodsmoke, roasting meat, fresh ale, and the bitter tang of vomit. The din of raucous laughter and shouts filled her ears.

Raised platforms, swathed in furs and blankets, lined the walls. Some were occupied by sleeping hirdmen, others by couples who were very much awake.

Her new companion seemed roused by the sight, reaching out to grab her.

'Not now,' she deflected, 'there's work to be done. My master will not be pleased if I tarry.'

He spun her around, his arms encircling her from behind. 'I won't take long.'

Reaching down, she gave his manhood a light squeeze. 'Oh, but I do!' She looked up at him, her smile wicked.

He released her, looking confused.

'Do you have a name, warrior? Or should I just call you Tor?' Gunnhild teased and stroked his upper arm.

The warrior laughed. 'Close. I am Torsten Birgersson of Stiklestad.'

Gunnhild flashed her most alluring smile. 'I'm Astrid. Seek me out tomorrow,' she promised, rising to kiss his cheek. 'Then we'll have plenty of time.'

Departing, she resumed her mission. The grand hearth blazed in the centre of the hall, surrounded by servants tending to pots and pans. Round tables were strewn about, each occupied by hirdmen, some seated, others sprawled on the straw-laden floor in drunken slumber.

Two men, each with more than fifty winters behind them, sat in high seats by the hearth. One, grey and balding, and the other with a short, dark mane—Sigrød and Halvdan the Black, she assumed.

Gunnhild grabbed a pitcher, sniffed its content to confirm

it was ale, and moved to the dark-haired man.

Passing a tapestry depicting a naval battle, she recognised the golden-haired warrior in the centre.

'King Fairhair,' she muttered under her breath, 'now I must clean up the mess you couldn't.'

As Gunnhild approached Halvdan, he was indulging in his ale, his horn tilted back as he took a long, leisurely drink. Unaware of the imminent danger, his attention was directed towards the revelries of his men. She moved past him, choosing to tend to Sigrød's empty horn first. It was a subtle diversion that further distracted the already inebriated Halvdan.

The action was a part of the routine, and neither leader paid her any special mind. She was a serving girl, a part of the scenery, meant to be seen but not noticed.

With a breath to steady herself, she took hold of Halvdan's horn. Her movements were calculated, even practised. With a swift flick of her wrist, she drained what little ale remained in Halvdan's horn on to the trodden floor below, unnoticed amid the chaos of the celebration.

Hiding her intentions under the guise of refilling his drink, she reached for the small flask hidden in her sleeve. With a quick, practised motion, she uncorked it, its deadly contents mixing seamlessly with the fresh pour of ale.

As soon as the horn touched the table, Halvdan's hand reached out and gripped it, bringing it to his lips. He drank deeply, oblivious to the danger he had just invited in. A sense of satisfaction washed over Gunnhild, a small victory in her risky endeavour.

As she turned her back on Halvdan, a strong hand seized her left arm.

'Who are you?' Halvdan the Black said, his face twisted with suspicion. 'I have not seen you before.'

Gunnhild cast a quick glance as Sigrød. The host, who was most likely to know about his slaves and servants, was engaged in conversation with two housecarls.

'I'm Astrid, my lord,' Gunnhild replied, and curtsied clumsily.

'From where do you hail?' Halvdan pressed, not letting go of her arm.

'From Sandnes in Håløygaland. But I served lady Bergljot at Lade until recently.'

Halvdan's eyes narrowed, as if he tried to look straight through her. 'Is there anyone here who can confirm your claims?'

Gunnhild straightened up and suppressed the urge to wriggle her arm loose from Halvdan's grip. 'Of course! My betrothed, Torsten Birgersson, is right there.' She pointed and waved at him with her free arm.

As she had hope, Torsten had had his eyes on her as she made her rounds. Now, he stood by his table a dozen paces away, looking distraught.

Halvdan let go of her arm. 'Who is she?' he called for Torsten to hear over the ruckus in the hall.

'Astrid!' Torsten replied, looking proud for remembering her name.

'Yours?' Halvdan continued.

Torsten's face broke into a wide grin. 'Oh, yes! She's mine!'

Gunnhild rewarded him with her warmest smile and turned back to Halvdan. She allowed her shoulders to relax and look at her husband's half-brother with practiced indifference. 'Do you need anything else?'

Without a word, Halvdan turned away from her and gave her a slight shove with the back of his hand

Gunnhild inhaled and pressed onwards, her heart pounding in her chest. She moved fluidly among the raucous men, her serving pitcher in hand, dispensing the golden liquid into waiting horns. Her senses were heightened, every boisterous laugh, every clank of metal, every smoky whiff from the hearth seemed to be magnified. She was walking a deadly tightrope, her fate hinged on every step she took, every word she spoke, every empty horn she refilled.

Gradually, the ale in her pitcher diminished, each pour a countdown to the end of her dangerous game. Her steps drew her to the man she had met outside, slouched in a corner, his eyes heavy with drink. In the flickering light, his face appeared softer, the harsh lines of a warrior's life smoothed out by the fog of inebriation.

She tilted her pitcher, the last of the ale trickling into his horn. As she straightened up, her eyes met his. There was a silent understanding that passed between them, a moment loaded with the weight of her unspoken intentions.

'Tomorrow,' she breathed, her hushed promise barely airborne before the surrounding clamour swallowed it.

His eyes held hers for a beat longer, a flicker of confusion dancing in their depths. Then he shrugged it off, raising his newly filled horn in a silent toast. He was unaware of the true meaning of her words.

Gunnhild moved away, leaving behind the promise of a tomorrow that would forever alter the realm. The die had been cast, and now, all they could do was wait consequences it would bring.

Leaving the empty pitcher where she had found it, she picked up a water bucket and left the hall. With a last glance behind to ensure nobody followed her, she slipped out the door. Once outside, she dropped the bucket and returned to her brothers by the pit house.

'Is it done?' Alv asked in a whisper.

'It is,' Gunnhild confirmed.

'We must make haste before something awry happens,' Øyvind suggested, his eyes anxiously scanning the longhouse.

'No rush,' Gunnhild retorted, 'Halvdan will remain

ignorant till we're back on our ship.'

CHAPTER: TIDINGS

Giske, Møre

On the windswept isle of Giske in Møre, Jarl Tore Teiande's face wore a look of surprise as he met the queen at the pier. 'Queen Gunnhild!' he greeted. 'Had I known of your arrival, I would have made the proper preparations.'

'Good evening, Jarl Tore,' said Gunnhild with a smile. 'No preparations are needed, save only some food and somewhere for my companions to sleep with shelter from the rain tonight.'

'Of course, my queen. How many are you?'

'Merely myself, my brothers, and a crew of six.'

'I shall have my steward make the arrangements,' Jarl Tore said. 'We were just about to have supper. Please, join me inside.'

'I appreciate your kindness, Jarl Tore,' replied Gunnhild, her voice softening with the encroaching dusk.

As they made their way from the pier, Tore extended his arm towards her, a silent offer of assistance on the uneven ground leading to his longhouse. After a few steps, he turned his head to look back towards the small ship at the shore.

'Ah, my brothers,' Gunnhild answered his unasked question, 'they prefer the company of our crew to the comfort of the longhouse.'

'Very well,' Jarl Tore said.

Soon after, they stepped into the stunning longhouse on the island of Giske, a seat belonging to the Jarls of Møre for generations.

'Ålov! The queen will share our meal with us,' Tore called.

A woman rose from her chair so fast that it tipped over. She turned to pick it up, but changed her mind and hastily flattened and adjusted her dress.

'My queen! Please forgive me for my attire! I have not heard a word of your coming!'

'Ålov! Such a pleasure to see you again,' Gunnhild said, her smile attempting to counter her host's evident displeasure at the surprise visit. 'How long has it been?'

'Three years, if my memory serves me right,' Ålov replied. 'Eirik was here the summer before last, but I believe you were with child and unable to travel.'

'Indeed, I was. And that summer was particularly unpleasant,' Gunnhild confirmed. 'But, speaking of children, is that your daughter by the hearth?'

Ålov turned to the young woman standing by their table. 'Yes, that is our Bergljot.'

Gunnhild walked towards the table to greet her. 'Such a pleasant surprise, Bergljot! I did not expect you to still live with your parents. Last I heard, you were betrothed to Jarl Sigurd Håkonsson of Lade.'

Bergljot's grimace marred her otherwise comely face. 'I am, but Sigurd has postponed the marriage because all my uncles are trying to kill each other. He fears our wedding might turn into a massacre.'

Gunnhild's lips formed a sympathetic pout. 'Indeed, Fairhair's sons are known for their belligerence. My heart goes out to you.'

'Our family has suffered worse at the hands of the Haraldssons,' Tore said.

'Really? I was under the impression that the jarls of Møre were always King Harald's loyal allies,' Gunnhild said.

'Indeed, we stood firm beside King Harald until the fateful

day when Halvdan Hålegg and Gudrød Ljome committed a terrible atrocity, burning my father and his men—five dozen strong,' Tore confessed, his tone hardening at the bitter memory.

A grimace of dismay crossed Gunnhild's face. 'I am truly sorry, Tore. I know not why this truth was kept from me.'

'It was many years ago, long before you were born,' Ålov said.

Gunnhild thought for some time, trying to remember her first conversation with King Harald. 'Halvdan and Gudrød were Snøfrid's sons?'

'That vile sorceress!' Ålov hissed.

'Ålov!' Tore rebuked her.

Ålov looked at Gunnhild and reddened. She opened her mouth to speak but seemed not to find the words.

'Fear not, Ålov,' Gunnhild said. 'I know many also believe *I* am a vile sorceress. I take no offence.'

'I'm sorry,' Ålov said.

'Don't be,' Gunnhild said with a smile. 'There can be advantages to having a reputation as a sorceress.'

'Please, Gunnhild, have a seat and share our food.' Tore offered his high seat for her to sit on.

Gunnhild accepted, and soon she had a plateful of food and a horn full of mead.

'Thank you for your hospitality, Tore,' Gunnhild said. 'But I must ask, what did Harald do when his atrocious sons murdered his friend Ragnvald?'

'Not much, I'm afraid,' Tore said. 'He chased down Gudrød, but reconciled with him and allowed him to withdraw to a modest estate in Agder. I haven't heard of him since.'

'He drowned, if my memory serves me correctly,' Gunnhild said.

'Did he? I didn't know that,' Tore said.

'And what about Halvdan Hålegg?' queried Gunnhild.

Tore sighed. 'Halvdan stole three of my father's ships and sailed to the Norðreyjar, or the Orkneys, as they're called now. He forced my brother Torv-Einar to flee, but he soon returned with a superior force and defeated Halvdan.'

'I'm happy to hear that. King Harald said Halvdan died on the Orkneys. I assume your brother slew him?'

'Indeed, he met his fate at Torv-Einar's hands. My brother executed the gruesome blood eagle on him, ripping open his ribs and yanking out his lungs,' Tore recounted, his words threaded with a hint of grim satisfaction.

A shudder passed through Gunnhild. 'The blood eagle,' she whispered, 'a ghastly yet fitting vengeance.'

'It was. In addition, King Harald granted Torv-Einar the dominion of the Orkneys, elevated me as the Jarl of Møre, and offered me his daughter's hand as restitution.'

'It sounds so romantic when you put it like that,' Ålov said.

Tore laughed. Neither of the women joined in.

'So, you are the jarl of Møre. Your brother Torv-Einar rules the Orkneys and your eldest brother Gange-Rolv rules Normandy? Your family has done well,' Gunnhild said.

'Perhaps,' Tore said. 'However, Rolv died last winter.'

'I'm sorry for your loss,' Gunnhild offered.

'Don't be. He was an old man, and I only met him a few times as a child,' said Tore.

Gunnhild turned her attention to the food, but before she had finished her plate, the door burst open, and a man stomped in with a servant on his heels.

'I beg your pardon, my lord,' the servant stuttered, wringing his hands in distress. 'I endeavoured to halt him, but my pleas fell on deaf ears.'

Jarl Tore rose and picked up a knife from the table.

The uninvited guest strode towards them. His hair and clothes were soaked, and his shoes made a sloshing sound with every step. Gunnhild recognised him the moment he spoke.

'Fear me not, Jarl Tore,' the man said. 'I have come for Queen Gunnhild.'

Tore looked to Gunnhild, who nodded.

'You have found me, Berg-Onund. What has happened?'

'The king has been struck with a grievous fever, my queen. We fear he may not see tomorrow. It's imperative that we set sail for Avaldsnes come daybreak.'

For a fleeting moment, time seemed to halt around Gunnhild. An icy knot of dread coiled in her stomach, swiftly snuffing out the comforting warmth of the mead and the fire. Her hands involuntarily clenched the edge of the table.

'The king …,' she whispered, her voice barely a thread of sound. The seriousness of the situation etched itself on to her face, her eyes reflecting the flicker of the firelight and a hint of rising fear.

'Prepare the ship,' she commanded, her voice regaining strength. 'We leave at first light.'

CHAPTER: MOUND

Karmøy, Rogaland

As dawn broke through the mist, Gunnhild discovered Eirik silhouetted against the colossal burial mound. With a silent grace, she weaved her fingers into his, leaning into his strength.

Eirik reciprocated, his grip tightening around her hand in comforting silence.

'Did you lay him to rest?' she finally asked, her voice hushed.

'No,' Eirik replied. 'My father had his rites prepared before he met his end. His faithful hirdmen carried him to his final rest two days past his demise.'

'Without a grand feast? Sacrifices? Harald was a monarch beyond compare.'

'Indeed, such ceremonies took place, but only in the presence of his hird and household.'

'But why was that?'

'He decreed that I was to be the king henceforth, and his departure was to be treated as a trivial matter.'

Gunnhild nodded in understanding. 'A strategy to deter rebellion.'

'Possibly. Yet, I fear it had little effect.'

'What news reach you?'

'Sigrød rallies his forces in Trøndelag. He plans to march southward to join forces with Olav in Viken,' Eirik said, turning to meet Gunnhild's gaze. 'News has also arrived that Halvdan the Black has left this world.'

'Indeed? And how did he meet his end?' Gunnhild asked, playing along with the ruse.

'He took ill the day following a feast at Sigrød's estate and succumbed on the following night.'

'A tragic loss.' Gunnhild feigned sympathy.

'A pity Sigrød did not meet the same fate,' Eirik retorted.

'Perhaps it is for the better. One man may fall ill and die, and it could pass as misfortune. But should his brother meet the same fate, it might be seen as a result of foul magic or poison.'

'Indeed, such occurrences would have sparked discontent,' Eirik conceded.

'With such suspicions, every warrior in Trøndelag would swear loyalty to Sigurd Ladejarl. His power would then match yours.'

Eirik nodded in agreement. 'What course of action do you suggest?'

'Do you now command your father's forces and fleet?'

'I do,' Eirik affirmed. 'Kjetil Hundolfsson presented his sword to me as a token of every man's fealty under my father's rule.'

A sombre expression passed over Gunnhild's face. 'Their loyalty is as fleeting as a ship passing in the night. You've seen how fortunes can change, how quickly the tides can turn.' Her words, though chilling, held a ring of truth.

She stepped closer to him, her voice dropping to a whisper. 'You must make your move while your might remains unchallenged, while your name still echoes with the weight of your father's legacy. Take the reins before someone else tries to.'

Eirik tightened his grip on her hand and turned to her, his eyes reflecting gratitude and resolve. 'I am fortunate, indeed, to have you by my side. Your wisdom shines brighter than any blade.'

'Indeed, you are,' Gunnhild replied, a slight smirk on her lips as she stood on her tiptoes to plant a kiss on her husband.

CHAPTER: TØNSBERG

Tønsberg, Viken, spring 934

Arinbjørn watched as several warriors emerged from the heart of Tønsberg, hurrying to join the ranks of their brethren forming a battle line on the open fields beyond the town. The air was laden with the scent of spring and the impending chaos of battle.

An opportune wind had allowed King Eirik's fleet of five longships to sail uninterrupted for days and nights. Their unexpected arrival caught the opposing forces of Olav and Sigrød off guard. Despite his long absence from the front lines, Arinbjørn found an odd calm within him. He realised his confidence was not just rooted in years of training and experience, but also in their superior numbers.

The touch of a hand on his shoulder drew his gaze upward. He was met with the stern countenance of King Eirik.

'I am ready,' declared the king, his voice as firm as the grasp on Arinbjørn's shoulder.

'No attempts at diplomacy?' Arinbjørn questioned, his eyes scanning over the enemy forces as they hastily assembled in formations.

'None. There is no room for negotiation. My brothers must die, and they are aware of this.' Eirik's words were cold, his eyes devoid of any hesitation.

'As you command, my king,' Arinbjørn replied, lifting his arm in preparation for what was to come. He took in a deep breath before raising his voice above the din of the assembled men. 'Silence! The king will speak!'

Like waves in still water, his words spread outwards from his position at the front line. A wave of quiet whispers and hushed murmurs washed over the ranks, silencing the sounds of chatter and clang of weaponry as six hundred warriors halted their preparations, turning their attention to their king.

Soon, the deep voice of King Eirik echoed over the hushed ranks. 'Kingsmen!' The response was immediate. A resounding clash of weapons against shields filled the air. Eirik waited for the racket to die down before he continued, his voice powerful and inspiring.

'You have already claimed the day!' His proclamation was met with a roar of approval from his men, a surge of pride and exhilaration sweeping through their ranks. Arinbjørn, however, found himself wincing at Eirik's unconventional method of rallying his men prior to battle.

'Through your relentless efforts, through sleepless nights and exhausting days, you've carried us here faster than anyone had predicted. Therefore, we face an enemy that is ill-prepared and outmatched. You will be victorious.'

His words were met with cheers, smiles and laughter, the kingsmen relishing their apparent advantage. Arinbjørn, despite his misgivings, could not help the slight shake of his head at the spectacle.

'And yet,' Eirik's voice rose above the din, commanding silence once again, 'this will be the hardest battle you've ever fought!'

The laughter died almost instantaneously. Every gaze was fixed on the king, their expressions varying from confusion to apprehension.

'The men you see before you are not mere peasants or fishermen. They are hardened warriors, veterans of numerous raids and battles. They know what fate likely awaits them, and still they choose to face us. They come prepared to die, ready to drag one of you with them to the hallowed halls of Valhall. They are fearless, undaunted and ruthless. Only by matching their fervour can we shatter their lines and end this battle before it claims the lives of our comrades.'

A chilling silence descended upon the army. Eirik's stern gaze swept over his men, his eyes finally landing on Arinbjørn. He raised his battle-axe, its blade gleaming ominously in the sunlight. Understanding the silent cue, Arinbjørn nodded and lifted his shield in response.

With a thunderous roar, King Eirik pivoted on his heel and charged towards the enemy lines, Arinbjørn trailing close behind. The ground beneath their feet trembled as the rest of the army followed suit, the air reverberating with the deafening clang of weapons and the pounding of their boots against the earth.

As they closed in on the enemy, Arinbjørn lifted his shield in preparation for the inevitable clash. Just a few paces ahead, he watched King Eirik deflect two incoming spears before launching himself shoulder-first into the enemy's shield wall. Steeling himself, Arinbjørn mimicked his king's actions. The enemy ranks wavered as the kingsmen threw themselves against them, their shields clashing violently against the defensive formation.

A sharp, sudden pain in his shoulder brought Arinbjørn's attention back to his immediate surroundings. Looking down, he found a spear embedded into his armour. Turning towards his attacker, he barely had time to react as his opponent pulled out the spear for another thrust.

Cursing, Arinbjørn managed to lift his shield just enough to protect his chest, but the spear scraped the edge of his shield and found its mark on his shoulder, not far from the first wound. Enraged, Arinbjørn dropped to his knees and rammed his shield into the enemy's thigh.

A cry of pain was his only response as his foe retaliated,

slamming his shield into Arinbjørn's helm. The impact sent him reeling, disorienting him. Struggling to lift his shield, he found his wounded shoulder failing him. Bracing himself for the impending blow, he closed his eyes.

A heavy weight landed on his right hand, followed by the unmistakable sound of bones crushing under the force. He could feel the weight on his shield increase as his enemy leaned over him, aiming for a fatal blow. But before he could react, the weight suddenly lifted, and a familiar voice rang out beside him.

'Get up, brother!' King Eirik called, his grip firm on Arinbjørn's upper arm. 'You can't win a battle sitting on your arse!'

Managing to get back on his feet, Arinbjørn glanced at his injured hand. It was smeared with dirt and blood, and the pain shot through his arm as he tightened his grip on his sword. 'Thank you,' he muttered, but Eirik had already moved on, assailing the remnants of the enemy's shield wall.

With the pressure of the kingsmen behind him, Arinbjørn had no choice but to follow suit, forcing himself into the enemy ranks. The shield wall disintegrated into chaos as the battlefield devolved into a close-knit, frenzied melee.

Arinbjørn soon found himself locked in combat with a skilled warrior. His sword was ineffective in the confined space, and he regretted not having drawn his seax for the close-quarters battle. As their struggle evolved into a grapple, Arinbjørn's wounded shoulder throbbed with every move. Running out of options, he headbutted his foe. The next moment, his opponent dropped to the ground with a fatal wound to the abdomen.

As the battle raged on, Arinbjørn caught sight of two prominent figures in the enemy's ranks—Olav and Sigrød. The sight spurred him to action. His injury was severe, and if they didn't end the battle soon, he'd be unable to continue fighting. With renewed vigour, he called out to his men, 'To me!' and directed them towards the enemy leaders.

As Arinbjørn's charge broke through the remnants of the defenders' ranks, the two rebel kings stood their ground. Arinbjørn engaged Sigrød, while Eirik took on Olav. The sound of steel clashing against steel echoed across the battlefield.

Engrossed in the fight, Arinbjørn parried Sigrød's attack. His shield splintered, forcing him to it. Changing tactics, he kept his distance and began to dodge and deflect the attacks, instead of blocking them. With each parry, a surge of pain shot through his injured hand, forcing him to focus more on evading the attacks.

He cast a quick glance at the side and noticed that the kingsmen were gaining ground. Sigrød must have noticed it too, for he launched an all-out attack, aiming his shield towards Arinbjørn's injured shoulder, followed by a low swing of his sword. But Arinbjørn managed to dodge both, seizing the opportunity to strike a blow to his foe's arm, causing him to drop his weapon. Wasting no time, he plunged his sword into Sigrød's chest.

Not far from him, Eirik and Olav were locked in their battle, neither gaining the upper hand. Eirik feinted left, narrowly missing Olav's neck with his axe with the following backhand strike. Olav counterattacked, but Eirik managed to deflect it with his shield. Taking advantage of the opening, Eirik struck his battle-axe through Olav's collarbone and into his rib cage, sending him lifeless to the ground.

The demise of Olav and Sigrød was devastating to the morale of the enemy. Their forces, once a united front of seasoned warriors, now crumbled under the weight of the loss of their leaders, and the rebels who had stood ground mere moments ago began to scatter.

Arinbjørn watched the unfolding scene, his gaze firmly set on the fleeing enemy warriors. He turned to Eirik, seeking guidance for their next move. 'Should we pursue them?'

Eirik, standing tall and resolute, shook his head. His eyes still fixed on the dissolving enemy ranks, he said, 'No, let them go. They pose no threat any more.' His voice was filled with confidence.

At the king's orders, Arinbjørn nodded, the signs of exhaustion beginning to show on his battle-hardened face.

'You should have someone look at that shoulder,' Eirik said, his tone soft yet firm.

'I will,' Arinbjørn replied, 'but first, we need to deal with our victorious army.'

Eirik's gaze scanned the battlefield. 'For now, they are busy tending to the wounded and looting the dead.'

'And afterwards,' Arinbjørn asked, 'will you allow them to pillage Tønsberg?'

'No,' Eirik stated firmly, 'Tønsberg is under my rule and protection.'

'Your men won't be happy leaving empty-handed, my king.'

'They won't,' Eirik agreed. 'Let them plunder Olav's estates and send the loot home with the wounded. The rest shall stay with me, here in Viken.'

'And how long do you plan to stay in Viken?' Arinbjørn asked, unable to hide his curiosity.

'We'll spend the summer here,' Eirik replied with a smile. 'We'll consolidate our rule, collect taxes, attend feasts and hand out gifts to those who remain loyal to me.'

Arinbjørn quirked an eyebrow. 'Ruling like your father?'

With a nod of affirmation, Eirik said, 'Just like my father.'

PART FIVE

Ting

CHAPTER:
INHERITANCE

Svanøy, Firdafylke, 934

'My lord, esteemed guests have arrived.' The voice echoed softly in the grand hall.

Arinbjørn paused to take a thoughtful sip of his ale, casually wiping his mouth with a worn cloth before slowly rising from his throne. 'At this hour? Who graces us with their presence?'

'Egil Skallagrimsson, my lord. Along with his wife,' came the clear reply.

'Very well, Borr. Bid them welcome and ensure they are offered refreshments.'

The grand doors of the hall swung open, and in strode the formidable Egil Skallagrimsson, with a woman maintaining a respectful distance behind him.

'An unexpected pleasure, old friend,' greeted Egil warmly.

'The delight is entirely mine,' Arinbjørn returned the greeting. 'Would you be so kind as to introduce your lady?'

Egil turned, gently taking the woman's hand. 'There's no need for formal introductions. You are already acquainted. Asgjerd, the widow of Torolv, and now my wife. Also, your cousin.'

Recognition dawned upon Arinbjørn instantly as he looked upon her face. 'Asgjerd! I had hoped our reunion to be under happier circumstances. I mourn Torolv's passing—he was a towering figure among men and a cherished ally.'

'Thank you, Arinbjørn,' Asgjerd responded softly.

'Do sit and share with me the tale of Torolv's demise,' invited Arinbjørn.

Egil began to narrate. 'My brother and I had been serving King Aethelstan in England. The previous year bore witness to a decisive battle at Vinheath. Aethelstan was victorious, but at the cost of Torolv's life.'

'I am deeply saddened by his passing. But he has secured his place at Odin's table,' Arinbjørn said.

'Indeed, he has,' Egil agreed solemnly.

A brief pause ensued as Borr, along with the maid Dagrun, arrived with replenished drinking horns and an array of food for the weary guests.

'Now, let's cut to the chase,' Arinbjørn urged after they were all seated. 'What brings an outlaw and enemy of the king to the Norwegian coast?'

'King Fairhair is no more, and I bear no ill will towards his son,' Egil declared.

Arinbjørn shot him a dubious glance. 'Perhaps. Yet his queen harbours a deep-seated hatred for you.'

Egil merely shrugged. 'I require your assistance.'

'How may I be of service?'

'To secure my rightful inheritance.'

Arinbjørn shot him a puzzled look, then glanced at Asgjerd. 'Explain!'

'I believe you are already familiar with much of the story,' Egil began, 'but you may not have given thought to its repercussions.'

Arinbjørn merely nodded for him to continue.

'Years ago, Bjørn Brynjolfsson married Tora, your father's

sister,' Egil reminded him.

'Without my father's consent, as I remember,' Arinbjørn interjected.

'True, at that time,' Egil agreed. 'They later made amends with your father and received a pardon from King Eirik.'

'Only after my father cleared their fines,' Arinbjørn added.

'Indeed,' Egil nodded, looking around the grand hall. 'Speaking of which, where might your father be?'

'He passed away two winters ago.'

'I am deeply sorry for your loss. Your father was a man of compassion and wisdom, much like yourself,' Egil offered.

Arinbjørn accepted the condolences with a soft, 'Thank you.'

There was a pause. Egil seemed lost in thought, perhaps unsure of how to continue after learning of Tore's death.

Asgjerd interjected, 'As you know, Bjørn Brynjolfsson was my father, who succumbed to a fever a few years ago.'

Arinbjørn turned to her expectantly. 'Yes?'

'After my mother passed away during my childhood, my father remarried Alof Erlingsdotter and had a daughter, Gunnhild. She later married ...'

'Berg-Onund Torgeirsson,' Arinbjørn filled in.

'Yes,' Asgjerd confirmed. 'Upon my father's death, Berg-Onund seized all of his lands and estates.'

Arinbjørn leaned back, absorbing the new information. 'I see.'

'Recently, I confronted Berg-Onund, staking a claim to half of Bjørn's inheritance, since Asgjerd is Gunnhild's sister,' continued Egil.

'That seems plausible,' Arinbjørn agreed. 'Did Berg-Onund accept your claim?'

'Quite the contrary!' Egil fumed. 'He denied Asgjerd any

right to the inheritance, claiming that since Bjørn had taken Tora without Tore's consent, their offspring had no rights. He even compared Tora to a runaway thrall!'

Arinbjørn visibly bristled at Berg-Onund's disrespectful comment about his aunt. 'And now, you wish for me to mediate with Berg-Onund on your behalf?'

'No, I seek an audience with the king to validate my claim,' stated Egil.

'I fear this may prove a difficult endeavour. Berg-Onund is King Eirik's trusted hirdman. He can be obstinate and difficult to reason with, and he enjoys significant support from both the king and the queen. Gunnhild, in particular, is your fiercest adversary. She may even plot your assassination upon learning of your return,' Arinbjørn warned.

Unfazed, Egil shrugged. 'She has made such attempts before—all in vain.'

'And if I fail to convince the king to support you?'

'Then, I shall take my claim to the Gulating.'

With a grave nod, Arinbjørn conceded, 'I shall do my utmost.'

CHAPTER: NEGOTIATIONS

Avaldsnes, Rogaland

'Arinbjørn!' hailed Eirik. 'Our hall has missed your presence. It's been an age since your last visit.'

Arinbjørn, adopting a bow he'd learnt from the Saxon traders, responded, 'Forgive my absence, my king. My father's passing has left much to oversee on Svanøy.' He nodded to Gunnhild and added, 'My queen.'

Gunnhild leaned back in her comfortable chair next to the high seat. They were in the audience chamber at Avaldsnes, the very place she had met King Fairhair for the first time many years ago.

'A dark cloud follows you, Arinbjørn,' she said.

'Your eyes are keen, my queen,' Arinbjørn said. 'I have some distressing news, and an irksome situation we must solve.'

'Let us hear the news first then,' Eirik said.

'Torolv Skallagrimsson is dead. He fell in battle in England.'

Gunnhild's heart dropped into her belly, spun around, whirling her guts into a tight knot. She tried to control her breathing, lest her husband notice her reaction. *Inhale. Exhale.*

'A warrior's death,' Eirik said, his voice coming from somewhere far away.

'A warrior's death,' Arinbjørn confirmed.

The news of Torolv's death struck Gunnhild harder than she'd ever imagine it could. *How long had it been? Five winters? Six? Inhale. Exhale.*

'And the irksome situation?' asked Eirik.

'Bjørn Brynjolfsson died some years ago,' Arinbjørn said.

'Yes?'

'Bjørn had two daughters. Gunnhild, who married Berg-Onund of Askøy. And Asgjerd, who married Torolv Skallagrimsson.'

Eirik grimaced. 'And?'

'Torolv was slain in battle, and Asgjerd's new husband sought my counsel,' Arinbjørn continued.

Gunnhild drew in a breath and released it slowly.

'And?' Eirik said.

'He demanded half of Bjørn Brynjolfsson's lands and estates.'

'From whom?'

'From Berg-Onund,' Arinbjørn said.

'What does Berg-Onund think of this?'

'He refused. That's why Asgjerd's new husband came to me for help.'

'Who is this second husband who makes such bold claims?'

'Egil Skallagrimsson.'

Gunnhild heaved for air and squeezed her chair so hard her knuckles whitened. 'You should have his head for this!' she hissed.

'Your feelings for the Icelander are well known, my queen,' Arinbjørn said. 'But you cannot easily refute Egil's claims. Asgjerd is Bjørn Brynjolfsson's heiress, whether you like it or not.'

'Bjørn ran off with Tora like a thief in the night! Your

father never sanctioned their union,' Eirik spat.

'Yes, he did, on the same day Torolv gave you his longship on Svanøy. I was present when my father was reconciled with Bjørn and consented to his marriage with Tora Lacehand. And I was present years later, when my father gave his approval to Torolv Skallagrimsson's union with Asgjerd. I was even present when my father paid the fines for the men whom Egil slew at Atløy. Right is right, and law is law, my king.'

'Arinbjørn, you have long been a champion of Egil's cause,' Eirik began, his voice taut with frustration. 'In deference to our friendship, I have tolerated this obstinate savage within my realm, free from pursuit. But it grieves me to learn of your support for his affronts against my allies.'

Arinbjørn nodded. 'If this is your stance, Egil will take his case to the Gulating.'

'What difference does it make?' Eirik asked. 'I'm the king, and I oversee the Gulating and every other Ting in my realm.'

Arinbjørn sighed. 'No, my king, you don't. Your role at the Ting is to ensure the proceedings go according to our laws and traditions. You are not there to make your own decisions.'

'You must not yield to this madness!' Gunnhild urged, her voice resonating with such vehemence that filled the royal chamber. Her hands clenched into fists as her eyes bore into her husband's. 'That monstrous creature will not stop at mere inheritance! Egil is a storm, a maelstrom waiting to consume everything you hold dear. He will rend your realm apart, tearing through the bonds of kinship, tradition and law. He seeks not just land, but power, and his hunger is insatiable.'

She leaned forward, her voice dropping to a barely audible whisper, her eyes wide and filled with dread. 'I sense a terrible fate brewing at the heart of his intentions. It bodes ill, I tell you, Eirik! Ill for us, for our sons, for our rule. This isn't merely a matter of lands and legacies anymore. It's a storm gathering, threatening to wash us all away in its tide. We cannot—we must not—give him a chance to bring forth such devastation!'

CHAPTER: THE GULATING

Guløy, Sogn

The tension was thick as honey in the Gulating court. Gunnhild's heart pounded within her chest as the formidable Icelander, Egil Skallagrimsson, advanced. His fiery spirit and fearsome reputation were as towering as his presence.

The court was an intricate arrangement of hazel poles, bound by twisted veband ropes, forming a sacred space for the thirty-six judges. Arinbjørn had chosen the twelve from Firdafylke, while his kinsman, Tord Brynjolfsson, picked those from Sogn. These twenty-four formed one unified party in all lawsuits, while the twelve from Hordaland voted independently.

Even with a favourable court composition, Gunnhild couldn't shake her dread. Egil was an unpredictable force in any situation.

Egil's voice thundered, silencing the murmuring crowd.

'Give ear, honourable men and esteemed judges of the Gulating! Decide this suit in accordance with your revered laws. My wife, Asgjerd, is the rightful daughter of Bjørn Brynjolfsson and Tora Lacehand Roaldsdotter. Her noble lineage is beyond dispute. Yet her father's lands and estates have been unjustly claimed by Berg-Onund Torgeirsson, her sister's husband. I ask you to confer to Asgjerd her rightful share of her father's inheritance.'

Egil offered a slight nod before he returned to his

housecarls. Gunnhild felt a temporary reprieve as Egil withdrew without any malice in his words or actions, a rare occurrence.

Berg-Onund retaliated quickly.

'My wife, Gunnhild, is the true daughter of Bjørn,' Berg-Onund declared, his voice echoing in the court. 'His lawful wife was Alof, and thus Gunnhild is the rightful heir. For this, I claimed the property left by him.'

His gaze swivelled towards Egil, a fierce challenge burning in his eyes.

'This Asgjerd claims an inheritance that is not hers. She is the offspring of a captured woman, dragged from her homeland against her will. Egil, you believe that your brute force and cunning ways justify your claims. This time, you'll find the currents of fortune turning against you. I'll present irrefutable evidence to our respected king and revered judges: Asgjerd's mother, Tora Lacehand, was taken captive twice. When Asgjerd was born in the distant land of Iceland, both her parents were outlaws by royal decree.'

Berg-Onund turned back to the judges, his voice heavy with scorn.

'This impudent Icelander, despite the undeniable facts, dares to oppose the commands of King Eirik. Firstly, he sets foot again on our lands, ignoring the royal decree of exile. Secondly, he defends the rights of a bondwoman's child to claim an inheritance. I insist that the inheritance belongs rightfully to my wife and ask you to declare Asgjerd the bondwoman of the king.'

Arinbjørn strode into the court, his face burning with indignation, his voice shaking the still air. 'I present to the court twelve steadfast men, all of whom bore witness to the reconciliation of Tore and Bjørn, stand ready to pledge their solemn oaths before the king and the esteemed judges of the Gulating.'

As the judges retreated into deliberation, time seemed to

stretch. The silence was finally broken by a judge. 'Their oaths stand, unless the king decrees otherwise.'

Seemingly cornered, King Eirik responded hesitantly, 'I shall neither forbid nor allow.'

Gunnhild's eyes darted towards Eirik, her voice slicing through the thick tension. 'A great wonder is this, my king, that you allow this brute to make a mockery of the Gulating before your eyes. Would you even speak up against him if he lay claim to your kingdom of Norway?'

Egil rose, his voice boomed over the court.

'Bondwoman born this knave,
my brooch-decked lady calls.
Shameless in selfish greed,
such dealing Onund loves.
Braggart! My bride is one,
born heiress, jewelled dame.
Our oaths, great king, accept,
oaths that are meet and true.'

The crowd held its breath, each word from Egil was a jab at the king's authority.

Gunnhild's fury boiled over. Summoning her brother Alv, she commanded, 'Take your men and ensure justice is served.'

Alv's men sprang into action, cutting the ropes and lifting the hazel poles. The Ting erupted in disapproval, but the crowd, unarmed, had no choice but to bear witness the proceedings.

Egil stood towering above the fray. His voice rolled out like thunder, commanding the attention of the court.

'Queen Gunnhild, this court is not your feasting hall where you can wave your hand and have your whims executed. This is a sacred space where justice is determined, and the law respected.'

The assembled crowd held its breath, daring not even to whisper, for fear of missing the Icelander's words.

'Alas, the noble king is trapped in silence, while his queen tears apart the fabric of our customs and traditions. The high justice of Norway is disrupted, scorned and toyed with by a queen drunk with power.'

Egil turned his gaze towards the King Eirik. 'Lord, it is not the throne that grants authority, but the integrity and justice you demonstrate to your people. You have the power to correct this wrong.'

King Eirik remained silent, his face concealing any emotion or thought like a mask.

Gunnhild rose to her feet, her eyes blazing with indignation. Yet, her voice came out steady and cold. 'And who are you, Egil Skallagrimsson, to lecture us on law and justice? You, an outlaw and a murderer. You defy the king's edict and dare to question our authority?'

In reply, Egil only smiled, a chilling smile that did nothing to dispel the tension in the air. His voice rose above the others.

'Berg-Onund! Can you hear my words?'

'I hear you!' Berg-Onund replied.

'I challenge you to *holmgang*, to fight me here at the Ting. Let the victor have this property, both lands and chattels. I give you the chance to settle this dispute as a man, and I will call you a coward and a *nithing* should you refuse.'

Dread filled Gunnhild as reality sunk in. Few dared to cross swords with the formidable Egil Skallagrimsson and live to tell the tale. For Berg-Onund, Eirik's seasoned hirdman, the grim choice was now between a bitter end, or a life stained with dishonour.

However, King Eirik now intervened.

'If you, Egil Skallagrimsson, prefer to settle this dispute by fighting, I will grant you this.' King Eirik rose from his high seat and called to his men. 'Fetch my axe and my shield from the ship!'

'No!' Egil replied. 'I have seen enough of the king's ways and his sense of justice to have any hopes of a fair duel. On equal terms and numbers, I would not hesitate to take any challenge, but I will not fight a king's power or sacrifice my men against an overwhelming force.'

Now, Arinbjørn approached Egil. 'Come, Egil. There is nothing you can gain here. Let me escort you to your ships.'

With this, Arinbjørn took Egil by the arm, leading him away with thirty of his men for protection.

But Egil tore himself free and shouted for everyone to hear,

'Let this be known, among jarls and hersirs, and every man and woman in this realm, that I ban anyone from living on or gaining from the lands that belonged to Bjørn Brynjolfsson! I ban them from you, Berg-Onund, and from all others, natives and foreigners, high- or low-born. Any offender shall be denounced as a lawbreaker, a peace breaker, and accursed!'

The uproar from the crowd followed Egil and Arinbjørn as they made their departure. Yet, both men walked away with quiet resolve.

Gunnhild turned to Eirik, her voice was laced with venom. 'You cannot let him simply walk away, Eirik! After all the audacity he has shown! He should be seized at once!'

Eirik remained silent for a moment longer. When he finally spoke, his voice was calm yet authoritative. 'No, Gunnhild. Enough. You have already disrupted the Ting's peace with armed men. We have crossed the boundary of our laws and customs today. I must stay here to ensure that the Ting is properly closed before I can give chase.'

His gaze then shifted to Kjetil Hundolfsson. 'Have someone follow Egil and his men, and ready my fastest ships. We will set sail as soon as I have closed the Ting.'

CHAPTER: NITHING POLE

Avaldsnes, Rogaland

Each torturous day felt like a lifetime unto itself for Gunnhild. Following the tumult of the Gulating, she sought refuge in the familiar confines of Avaldsnes, accompanied by those of Eirik's men, who had not joined in the chase after Egil Skallagrimsson.

In the innocent mirth of her youngest sons, Erling and Gudrød, she found fragile solace, yet her mind remained unfocused and constantly wandered. Her five eldest sons, Gamle, Guttorm, Harald, Ragnvald and Ragnfrød were fostered by Eirik' loyal hersirs, as was her daughter Ragnhild. It had been six weeks since her last bleeding, and she felt certain it would be another son. Eirik's line was secure, but his realm was slipping through his fingers.

'My queen,' Astrid's voice sliced through the fog of Gunnhild's contemplation like a beacon, 'the king has returned.'

Those words, so long yearned for, triggered a rush of relief within her. 'Finally!' Gunnhild exclaimed as she found her feet with a swift motion, quickly swaddling herself in her cloak. 'Look after my sons for me!'

'As you command, my queen,' Astrid responded with a gentle nod.

Before departing, Gunnhild enveloped Sigurd in a fleeting embrace. With a quick pivot, she dashed towards the door.

She found Eirik in the high seat of his audience chamber, absorbed in examining a stave resting on his lap without acknowledging her arrival.

'Eirik!' Gunnhild rushed to him, her voice vibrating with urgency. 'A full week has passed! My dreams have been dark and full of terrors. I've been fearing some tragedy had befallen you!' She flung her arms around his neck, pressing her lips against his with a fervour that belied her worry.

Eirik's response was noticeably lacklustre.

'Much has befallen me, Gunnhild. And you.' Eirik's cryptic reply sent a chill down Gunnhild's spine.

'What? Enlighten me! And what is this?' Gunnhild questioned, her hand tentatively tracing the smooth surface of the stave nestled across Eirik's lap.

'This is a hazel pole. It was among those your brother ripped from the ground during the Ting. But there's much to be unravelled before we delve into that matter.' Eirik's voice was eerily hollow.

Gunnhild kept silent despite her inner turmoil, allowing Eirik to speak without interruptions.

'Most of Egil's fleet consisted of cumbersome merchant vessels, which allowed us to swiftly close in on them. However, he cunningly shuffled his finest warriors on to his fastest longship, leaving the remaining crews to their fate.'

'And what happened to them?' Gunnhild found herself asking, her hand darting to cover her mouth as she momentarily forgot her vow of silence.

'We slew every soul aboard. Some of those unfortunate men belonged to Arinbjørn's fold.'

When Gunnhild said nothing, Eirik continued.

'I chased him with my fastest ships and left the others behind. We had thirty-two oars to his eighteen, so we got ever closer. Kjetil Hundolfsson stood at the prow, close enough to count every man, when Egil threw a spear with so much force that half of the shaft poked out from his back. Kjetil was dead before he hit the deck.'

Gunnhild sucked in a mouthful of air and covered her mouth with both hands. Kjetil Hundolfsson had been the leader of King Harald's hird, a fair and capable man who would be sorely missed.

'Egil skilfully navigated his vessel into a narrow strait, its waters barely reaching knee-depth at low tide. The hull of his ship grated against the bottom as they rowed across the shallow passage, yet they managed to traverse it. My ship, laden with more men, possessed a deeper draft and we were forced to abandon our pursuit.'

'Did he escape?'

Eirik nodded. 'We sailed the long route around the island, but he eluded us. For days on end, we traversed the coast, scouring the waters for any sign of him. We believed he had set sail for Iceland. Perhaps he had, but the strong western wind might have deterred him from undertaking such a journey without adequate provisions. Therefore, he returned to our shores to restock and wait for more favourable weather.'

'How do you know this? Did you find him?'

Eirik shook his head.

'Egil made landfall on Askøy and sought out Berg-Onund's homestead at Fenring. Under the veil of darkness, he beguiled Berg-Onund into the depths of the forest and there he dispatched him, along with his brother Atle, as well as Frode and Hadd.'

'Oh, no!' Gunnhild wailed. She recalled fondly how Berg-Onund and Atle had been by Torolv's side when they discovered her in Finnmark; they held a dear place in her heart.

'Egil then led his men to Fenring and killed every man and woman of Berg-Onund's household who had not fled in time. Afterwards, they led the cattle to the shore and slaughtered them there. When they had loaded the meat on to the ship, they set sail for Iceland.'

'So they got away,' Gunnhild said, dejected.

'I wish it was so,' Eirik said, 'but soon after they left the shore, they spotted a smaller ship belonging to Skjegg-Tore. Onboard were a handful of survivors from Berg-Onund's estates, and six people who had feasted with Skjegg-Tore the night before.'

Gunnhild closed her eyes, but that did not stop the tears.

'Egil assailed the vessel, causing it to plummet beneath the waves. Those fortunate enough to escape the onslaught on the deck met their fate in the unforgiving sea. A single soul survived the carnage, a young maiden from Berg-Onund's stead.'

'An evil spirit resides in that man. I've known since the moment I first saw him,' Gunnhild said.

Eirik looked down at his hands.

'Is there more?' Gunnhild said, her heart picking up the pace.

Eirik nodded.

'Aboard that ill-fated vessel was Ragnvald, our son.'

At this revelation, a tumultuous surge of grief and rage made Gunnhild scream.

Eirik rose to his feet, his strong arms encompassing her fragile form. They remained intertwined until her screams gave way to quiet sobs, and the violent trembling subsided to a gentle tremor.

Summoning her resolve, Gunnhild gently extricated herself from Eirik's comforting embrace. An instinctual sense told her the tale was far from complete.

'And what of the pole?' She braced herself, her anticipation mingled with a trace of dread, unable to comprehend how this seemingly insignificant wooden object could hold such importance amid the tragedy.

Eirik extended the hazel pole to her. As she traced her fingers over the intricate markings etched into its surface, his words unfurled.

'Before Egil fled, he wedged this pole into a fissure in a rock on Herla Isle. He affixed a horse's head atop the pole, facing the mainland.'

Gunnhild's heart drummed a frantic beat against her ribcage as she deciphered the engraved inscription:

'*Here I erect a nithing pole and cast this curse upon King Eirik and Queen Gunnhild. I extend this same curse to the guardian spirits of this realm. May they all stray from their paths and never find their dwelling until they have ousted King Eirik and Gunnhild from these lands.*'

CHAPTER: RALLY

Avaldsnes, Rogaland, 935

Dark clouds loomed over Avaldsnes, mirroring the grim atmosphere that hung heavy in the great hall. King Eirik stood at the head of the long table, his fists clenched, and his gaze fixed on the flickering flames in the hearth.

'You summoned me, my king,' Arinbjørn said as he approached Eirik. 'My queen,' he added politely to Gunnhild, in her seat next to the throne.

'Thank you for coming so swiftly, Arinbjørn,' Eirik said. 'Please, have a seat and some ale.'

Arinbjørn complied and waited for Eirik to speak his mind.

'Haakon landed in Trøndelag with some of Aethelstan's warriors from England last summer,' Eirik said, his voice carrying an air of both frustration and determination. 'He has garnered the support of those who were loyal to Sigrød and Halvdan.'

Arinbjørn nodded, gauging the reactions of the king and queen. The tension was palpable, the fate of the kingdom hanging in the balance.

'We cannot underestimate Haakon's resolve,' Arinbjørn warned, his voice steady. 'He has been nurtured and trained in the court of King Aethelstan. He is a young man, but his ambitions are as fierce as his father's.'

Eirik turned to face Arinbjørn, his gaze burning with determination. 'I will not yield my birth right to Haakon or any other who seeks to claim what is mine. I am the rightful heir to the throne of Norway.'

Arinbjørn nodded in agreement. 'I stand by your side, my king, as I always have.'

Eirik's gaze shifted to Gunnhild, who merely nodded.

'We will gather our army and fleet,' he declared. 'Every loyal man and ship will answer the call. We sail north to meet Haakon on the field of battle before he can muster more support.'

Rising from her seat, Gunnhild stepped forward, her voice resolute. 'Our alliances must remain resolute,' she stated. 'Dispatch messengers to every loyal jarl, hersir and landholder who has sworn fealty to our cause. We require their unwavering support in this crucial moment.'

Eirik nodded. 'You are right, my queen. We need the support of our allies to overcome this threat.' He turned to Arinbjørn. 'Send messengers to remind them of the bonds we share.'

Gunnhild interjected, urgency in her voice. 'We must act swiftly. Haakon's arrival in Trøndelag may embolden others who question your claim to the throne. We must show them that we are resolute in our stance.'

Eirik's jaw tightened. 'I will not allow dissent to weaken our cause. We will show them the might of our army, the resilience of our spirit. Let it be known that we will defend our kingdom to the last man.'

A solemn silence enveloped the great hall as the winds outside howled, as if echoing the weight of the moment.

'When the storm subsides and the winds shift in our favour, we shall set sail for Trøndelag,' Eirik proclaimed, conviction in his voice. 'I shall vanquish Haakon and protect what is rightfully mine. Norway shall bear witness to the strength of its true king.'

CHAPTER: HAAKON

Giske, Møre

King Eirik hunched over the table, his gaze fixated on the rudimentary map of Trøndelag. 'Haakon has brought two hundred of Aethelstan's warriors from England,' he murmured. 'Coupled with those still loyal to Sigrød and Halvdan who rally under his banner, it's a formidable force, surpassing any we've previously encountered on the battlefield.'

Eirik looked up at Arinbjørn, who merely nodded.

'But my entire army is sailing north as we speak, and in two days, we sail for Lade. With support from Jarl Sigurd of Lade, we will have the upper hand against Haakon.'

'I would advise against placing too much trust in Jarl Sigurd's support against Haakon, my king,' Jarl Tore Teiande cautioned.

King Eirik furrowed his brow. 'Why do you say that? What do you know?'

Jarl Tore stared into his drinking horn while he spoke. 'My daughter Bergljot came to visit us one moon ago. She would not reveal much of her husband's plans, but from what little she did disclose I got the impression that Jarl Sigurd fully expected Haakon to return from England. I believe he has been preparing for his coming for some time.'

'This is outrageous! The jarls of Lade have always been loyal to my father and his kin!'

Gunnhild extended a comforting hand to rest on Eirik's tense shoulder, an effort he swiftly dismissed with a terse shrug.

'Sigurd Ladejarl is still loyal to your father's kin,' Tore said, squirming in his seat.

'What do you mean?'

'Young Haakon is Harald's son, just like you.'

'This is treachery! I'm the rightful heir of King Harald, not Haakon or any other bastard brother of mine!'

'So you say,' Tore said. 'However, you are not his only son, and not his firstborn. Some might argue that you have no more claim to the throne than any of your brothers.'

Eirik grabbed Jarl Tore by the shoulder. 'Are you, perhaps, one of those who doesn't support my claim to the throne?'

Tore swallowed but did not look away from King Eirik's stern gaze.

'No, my king, I'm merely letting you know how Jarl Sigurd and most men in Trøndelag think. Your father ruled with a firm hand and reduced the power of the wealthy farmers and chieftains. Many want to return to the old ways, and they believe Haakon will allow them to do just that.'

'They remain my subjects! They cannot simply barter their king for another at a whim.'

'And yet,' Arinbjørn interjected, 'that is what they are doing, whether we like it or not.'

Eirik let go of Tore. 'You, too?'

'I have always been loyal to you, Eirik,' Arinbjørn said, 'even when we disagreed. Even when you ignored my advice and opinion.'

Eirik reached for a piece of bread and ate it while he thought.

'With Sigrød and the twins slain, Sigurd Ladejarl now commands the resources and territories of three kings—the wealthiest and most densely populated regions within my realm,' he conceded, at long last.

Gunnhild and Arinbjørn looked at each other but said

nothing.

'And now Haakon arrives with hundreds of Aethelstan's warriors,' Eirik said.

Arinbjørn nodded.

'We must look elsewhere for support and raise an army superior to Haakon's and Sigurd's forces,' Eirik said.

'Where do you intend to find that support?' Arinbjørn said.

'Anywhere but Trøndelag!'

'Where?' Arinbjørn pressed.

Eirik glared at him.

'Håløygaland were ever loyal to the Jarl of Lade. You lost Viken when you killed your brothers Bjørn Farmann and Olav Haraldsson and spent a summer collecting taxes. And you lost the west after the debacle at the Gulating. Aethelstan has clearly taken Haakon's side,' Arinbjørn said.

'The Danes!' Eirik said. 'My mother was the daughter of King Eirik of Hedeby.'

'Perhaps,' Arinbjørn said. 'Provided they would commit their forces to the far north and risk an attack from England.'

'I cannot win this war,' Eirik said.

Gunnhild, Arinbjørn and Tore kept quiet.

Eirik nodded. 'Now I understand what Aethelstan tried to achieve.'

'What do you mean?' Tore said.

'I have corresponded with King Aethelstan since before my father died. Lately, he has insisted I come to England and serve as his underking in Jórvik. I considered the offer an insult.'

'Why would he do that?' Arinbjørn said.

'I did not know back then. But now, it seems he tried to make it easier for Haakon to seize the throne.'

'And he offered you an alternative?' Arinbjørn asked.

Eirik shrugged. 'So it seems.'

'Could there be other reasons?' Gunnhild said.

'Yes,' said Eirik, 'Aethelstan wrote that the kings of Wessex have never been able to rule the Danelaw. He reasoned the Danes would prefer a Norwegian king over any Saxon ruler he tried to instate in Northumbria.'

'That might be true,' Arinbjørn said.

'But what options do we have? I can't just disembark on some Northumbrian beach and declare myself their king. I'm unsure if Aethelstan was genuinely trying to draw me away from Norway or simply attempting to ensnare me in Northumbria, similar to the fate that befell Ragnar Lodbrok in days gone by.'

'If I may, my king?' Tore said.

'Yes?'

'My brother Torv-Einar is the jarl on the Orkney Islands. I can arrange for him to receive you and accommodate your family and your army until you have reached an agreement with Aethelstan.'

Eirik looked to Gunnhild, then to Arinbjørn.

'I don't see better alternatives, unless you would rather die a glorious death on a battlefield in Trøndelag. You would not be the first king to do so, and probably not the last.' Arinbjørn said.

'There will be time enough for you to find a battlefield to die on,' Gunnhild said. 'But our sons are not yet of age, and should you die now, they will be condemned to a lifetime of persecution and exile.'

'This was not what my father wanted when he named me his heir,' Eirik said.

'Your father sired two dozen rivals and sent Haakon to be raised and trained by Aethelstan,' Gunnhild said. 'Harald had to fight to retain his father's kingdom, and he kept fighting until he had conquered all of Norway. Your situation is not much different from his.'

'But I can't take my entire army to the Orkneys. Come autumn, most will return to their farms and their families.'

'Some will stay,' Arinbjørn said, 'and the Orkneys provide a perfect for trade and plunder. Take a few years to build your wealth and recruit men from the Norse populations in Northumbria and Ireland.'

'You can carve out your own realm abroad, like my brother Rolv did in Normandy,' Tore said.

'You've always had an innate tendency towards conquest rather than the intricacies of rule,' Gunnhild observed, her fingers gently tracing a reassuring path up his tensed arm. This time, there was no reflexive jerk, no instinctual rebuffing of her comforting touch.

'Is this truly the path you envision for me?' His voice echoed through the silent room, carrying a hint of uncertainty that was seldom heard from the self-assured king. There was an unusual vulnerability etched into the rugged lines of his face, a side that he rarely allowed to surface.

'Indeed, it is, Eirik,' Gunnhild responded, her tone the perfect blend of resoluteness and tenderness.

Eirik released a weary sigh, his gaze drifting momentarily to the crude map sprawled across the table before returning to Gunnhild's unwavering presence.

Gunnhild's fingers traced a path along the contours of his arm. 'Power alone cannot sustain a kingdom, Eirik. It requires the skilful governance and the delicate art of diplomacy.'

Eirik's brow furrowed as he grappled with the weighty implications of their conversation.

'What you suggest is the way of a spineless coward!' Eirik said. 'It was never my father's way, and it is certainly not my way.' He slammed his fist into the massive table.

Anger surged inside Gunnhild, but she looked down and

kept silent. Confronting Eirik while he was in this state would only make things worse.

With a wordless roar of frustration, Eirik turned on his heels and stomped towards the doors.

Gunnhild waited until he reached the doors before she spoke.

'Eirik,' she said, her voice soft and gentle.

Eirik stopped in the doorway but did not turn to face her.

'You will meet your end valiantly in the battleground, and your reception in Valhall will be like nobody else's. But should you fall, I will be drowned in a bog somewhere. And your sons will face destinies not preferable to mine. Why are you in such a haste to end our lives in Midgard?'

Eirik visibly deflated, but after a few heartbeats he left without closing the doors.

'What now?' Arinbjørn asked.

'We wait for Eirik to calm down and reach the obvious conclusion,' Gunnhild replied.

'Will he?'

'Sooner or later, unless his hand is forced before he gets there.'

Arinbjørn turned to Tore Teiande. 'Is the situation really this dire?'

Jarl Tore nodded. 'Young Haakon arrived last summer and spent the winter befriending the men of Trøndelag. He has promised to reverse some of the rules imposed on them by your father, for which he has won much support. His fondness for the White Christ has not gone down well with everybody, but it has not caused any serious problems.'

'Can we use that to drive a wedge between him and his allies?' Arinbjørn asked.

Tore sighed. 'We could. I know of at least half a dozen hersirs in Trøndelag eager to oust Haakon from the realm. I've met with some of them already and done what I can to support them. But the unfortunate events at the Gulating have given King Eirik the reputation of a tyrant, even in the west, and many are afraid to speak up on his behalf.'

Gunnhild felt a pang of guilt at the mention of the Gulating. She had lost her temper, as she always did in the presence of the vile Icelander. Nothing could be done about that now, however. She found her seat and leaned back, waiting for her husband to reach a decision.

The two others followed suit, and they shared a light meal in relative silence.

Before nightfall, Eirik returned. His steps were slow and heavy as he approached. He held up his hand, signalling for the others to remain seated.

'To embark upon a path of exile, to establish a realm beyond these shores … it is a daunting prospect,' Eirik confessed, his voice tempered with apprehension. 'But perhaps that is where I might forge a legacy worthy of my heritage.'

Gunnhild rose to provide her unwavering support, infusing her voice with conviction. 'In the land of Northumbria, you have the opportunity to build a kingdom of might and prosperity. You can mould your own destiny, free from the constraints of Trøndelag's treacherous politics.'

Eirik nodded, a flame of determination rekindled within his eyes. 'Then so be it. We shall set sail to the Orkneys and raise an army for the conquest of Northumbria.'

PART SIX

Northumbria

CHAPTER: JÓRVIK

Jórvik, Northumbria, 939

Eirik surveyed the walled city from a vantage point just beyond the reach of any archers atop the city walls. 'How many men do we have?' he inquired, his gaze fixed upon the formidable structure before them.

Arinbjørn hesitated for a moment, then responded, 'A few hundred.'

Eirik's steely gaze met Arinbjørn's, his silence carrying an unspoken demand for a more precise answer.

'More than two hundred, less than three,' Arinbjørn added.

Eirik's expression remained unyielding. 'Not enough,' he declared, his voice tinged with frustration. 'If there is a garrison within those walls, our chances of capturing the city with such a limited force are slim.'

'We must rely on the possibility of the gates being opened for us,' Arinbjørn suggested. 'Shall we proceed?'

Eirik's resolve hardened, his voice carrying a resolute tone. 'Let us forge ahead,' he commanded, determination etched upon his face.

Shouldering the weight of anticipation, the two warriors strode towards the formidable stone walls of Jórvik on foot, leaving their army behind with the ships. The imposing city gates loomed before them, protected by armed men positioned atop the wall. A distant tower rose high above the fortifications.

Nervous glances passed between Arinbjørn and the watchful guards.

Arinbjørn's voice quivered with uncertainty as he voiced their unspoken question, 'Will they grant us entry?'

Eirik's gaze remained fixed upon the gates as he responded with a quiet resolve, 'We shall soon find out.'

In hushed silence, they advanced, closing the distance until they stood thirty paces from the massive double doors that remained closed. Arinbjørn prepared to proclaim his lord's arrival, but Eirik's firm hand upon his shoulder halted his motion. With regal bearing, Eirik stepped forward, commanding the attention of the defenders, his voice resonating with authority and conviction.

'I am Eirik Haraldsson. By the decree of King Aethelstan, I have been named the ruler of Jórvik. I implore you to open these gates and allow me to assume my rightful position as your lord and protector.'

Silence enveloped them, the weight of expectation pressing upon their hearts. 'What shall we do?' Arinbjørn whispered, his voice fraught with uncertainty.

'We wait,' Eirik responded with unwavering determination.

Time seemed to stretch as they stood in suspense, their hopes resting on the gates before them. Then, as if responding to the unspoken plea, the massive doors groaned open, granting passage to a single figure. Draped in resplendent purple garments adorned with intricate embroidery, the man exuded an air of distinction. Neatly groomed hair, streaked with shades of grey, added to his dignified appearance.

'I am Archbishop Wulfstan. On behalf of the people of Eoforwic, I extend a warm welcome to you, Eric Haraldsson,' the archbishop announced, his nod acknowledging Arinbjørn in passing.

Wulfstan turned and beckoned the Northmen to follow

him. The heavy gates swung open at his command, held steadfast by four guards clad in chain mail armour. As the trio entered the city, Arinbjørn cast a backward glance, witnessing the closing of the gates behind them, sealing their fate within these unfamiliar walls.

'We are at their mercy,' Arinbjørn murmured, his voice barely audible.

Eirik's gaze remained fixed ahead. 'We have been for some time.'

Arinbjørn turned his attention to the city, his gaze sweeping over the narrow streets that stretched ahead. Timber buildings with thatched roofs dominated the landscape, but intermingled among them were larger stone and brick structures boasting tiled roofs. The houses and shops stood shoulder to shoulder, their upper stories projecting out over the lower levels, creating an architectural tapestry that seemed to defy gravity. Although the streets appeared deserted, curious eyes peered out from behind curtains and half-closed shutters, observing the arrival of these strangers.

Eirik's curiosity was aroused by the emptiness that greeted them. 'Where is everybody?' he wondered aloud. 'I was told there are nearly ten thousand people in this city.'

Wulfstan offered a courteous response, tinged with an apology. 'My lord, many deemed it wise to remain indoors or seek refuge with their kin rather than confront the formidable Eric Bloodaxe face to face. Your reputation precedes you, as they say.'

A wry smile crept on to Eirik's face. 'I am pleased to know that I have brought something with me from Norway, even if it is nothing more than an ill-famed reputation.'

'Indeed,' Wulfstan replied, a hint of amusement in his voice. 'As reputations tend to do.'

As they continued their journey through the city, Wulfstan gestured with a practised hand, drawing attention to two men dressed in attire similar to his own, though adorned in sombre grey instead of the luxurious purple. Adjacent to them stood a towering stone structure, its entrance adorned with a cross-shaped window.

Arinbjørn and Eirik exchanged knowing smiles. They had encountered such buildings during their raids, often finding them to be repositories of wealth.

'A place of worship, perhaps?' Arinbjørn queried.

'Ah, yes,' Wulfstan confirmed. 'Despite the profane heathen traditions, our Lord maintains a strong presence in our magnificent city. We boast ten churches, and our cathedral stands as the grandest north of the Humber. It lies just around the corner.'

A moment later, they stood in awe before a towering stone edifice, resplendent with stained-glass windows, golden crosses, and intricately carved stone embellishments.

'This is the cathedral of Eoforwic,' Wulfstan declared, his voice tinged with palpable pride. 'And to the right, your eyes shall feast upon the king's palace.'

Arinbjørn and Eirik turned their gaze, beholding a sprawling and imposing structure. Multiple buildings, crafted from an enigmatic blend of wood, stone and marble, encircled a central courtyard or hall. Carvings and ornate details adorned every surface, blending familiarity with an exotic allure.

Passing through an ancient stone gate that stood without doors, they entered a great hall that bore a resemblance to those found in their homeland, albeit fortified with solid stone foundations.

'That, King Eric, is your great hall,' Wulfstan explained. 'To the left, you will find your living quarters, and to the right, the courtyard, barracks and stables are at your disposal.'

Amid the bustling activity of men ferrying supplies and belongings between the buildings, a sense of unease lingered in the air. Some cast uneasy glances in their direction, while others hurriedly scurried out of their path.

'I beg your forgiveness, my lord,' Wulfstan apologised. 'Your predecessor hastily departed when news of your ships sighting on the River Ouse reached his ears. We have not yet had the opportunity to tidy up after his departure.'

Eirik's smile held a glimmer of amusement. 'I have seen worse, Wulfstan. And fear not, my wife remains in the Orkneys until I send for her.'

The mention of Eirik's wife piqued Wulfstan's curiosity. 'Ah, your wife ... Gunnhilda,' he remarked.

Eirik's interest was piqued. 'Yes?'

'I look forward to making her acquaintance,' Wulfstan said, a twinkle in his eye.

Eirik raised an eyebrow, a mischievous grin forming on his face. 'Ah, my wife has a reputation as well?'

Wulfstan chuckled. 'Indeed she does.'

Eirik's grin widened. 'Is it as flattering as mine?'

Wulfstan's laughter echoed through the corridors. 'Perhaps not quite.'

Eirik let out a hearty laugh. 'You can make up your own mind soon enough. But tell me, Archbishop, who built this remarkable city? I have never seen anything quite like it.'

Wulfstan paused, relishing the opportunity to share his knowledge. 'The Romans laid the initial foundations, followed by the Saxons. The Norwegians and the Danes left their mark as well. Each era left its imprint, and the city grew in accordance with the customs and traditions of its conquerors.'

Eirik's eyes sparkled with intrigue. 'I might just find myself at home here.'

Arinbjørn interjected, reminding them of the pressing matter at hand. 'And what of our army, Archbishop? Where shall they be accommodated?'

Wulfstan reassured them, his tone jovial. 'Fear not, my

lord. The barracks can house some of your men, and those with families might find vacant houses within the city. Alternatively, they can settle outside the city walls and build their own dwellings. Our people harbour no aversion to the presence of an army. In fact, in these lands, a vigilant army is not just welcome, but expected. Northumbria has never lacked its share of enemies.'

Eirik nodded, a sense of relief washing over him. 'Very well, then. Lead the way, Archbishop. It is time for me to meet with the ealdormen and begin the task that lies before us.'

CHAPTER: PALACE

Gunnhild set foot on the cobblestoned streets of Jórvik with a mixture of curiosity and trepidation. Eirik had spoken of its splendour, but it was one thing to hear the words and another entirely to experience the grand city first-hand. She noticed the details in the timber buildings, stone structures and cobbled streets, while her mind compared them to her homeland. All around her were Northumbrians, their accents strange and lilting to Gunnhild's ears. Their gazes were respectful but guarded, as if they were uncertain of what to make of their new queen.

Her guard, handpicked men from Norway, escorted her through the twisting streets of the city. Their Norse voices were a comforting familiarity among the otherwise foreign surroundings.

Her new abode loomed ahead. The king's palace, a sprawl of buildings carved from wood and stone, was an architectural marvel. As she walked through the gates, she couldn't help but admire the artistry that had gone into the structure. Its stone foundations, carved timber beams, and ornate designs were testament to a blend of cultures and craftsmanship.

Inside, the great hall was spacious and open, more elaborate than anything she had seen in Norway. Gunnhild was captivated by the high ceiling and intricately carved stone walls. She ran her hands across the carved reliefs on the wall, feeling the stories of old engraved in their lines. The wide central hearth was ablaze, casting a warm, comforting glow against the stone walls and woodwork.

Then, among the crowd, her gaze found Eirik. He stood with an aura of authority near the imposing high seat, his stature reflecting his power. He was conversing with a group of unfamiliar men, but at her entrance, he turned, his eyes finding hers across the hall.

A warm smile spread across his face as he excused himself from the group and strode towards her. There was a familiarity in his steps, a rhythm that she had known for years. Yet there was something new about him. He was King Eirik, again.

'My queen,' Eirik greeted her, his voice ringing with genuine warmth as he smiled at her.

He extended a hand as she approached, and she placed hers in his.

'I've missed you, Eirik,' she responded, her voice steady yet soft.

His grip tightened around her hand and their eyes locked on each other's.

'No kiss?' Gunnhild asked in a whisper.

'Later, surely,' Eirik said with a smile. 'There is someone I want you to meet.'

He led her to the hearth, where an elderly man in splendid robes waited patiently for them. 'This is Archbishop Wulfstan, the spiritual advisor to our court and the voice of Christ's church here in Jórvik,' Eirik introduced.

Wulfstan, imposing in his religious garb, approached Gunnhild with a cordial smile. His grey eyes held a hint of curiosity as he met her gaze.

'Welcome to Jórvik, Queen Gunnhilda,' he said, his voice carrying a touch of warmth that contrasted with the steely gaze.

'Thank you, Archbishop Wulfstan,' she responded, maintaining her composed demeanour. Her own gaze didn't waver from his.

'I trust your journey was uneventful?' he continued,

clasping his hands together. His posture exuded polite interest, but there was a calculating look in his eyes.

'As uneventful as a voyage can be,' Gunnhild replied. She put a hint of playfulness in her tone, a gentle prod at his formalities. She was here to rule, not to fit into his expectations.

He laughed lightly, nodding in understanding. 'I suppose sea voyages are their own breed of adventure,' he conceded with a smile.

'Indeed,' she responded, matching his smile. 'And now I am ready for the adventure of ruling Jórvik.'

There was a moment of silence as they both measured the implications of her words. Their polite exchange was a dance, a careful exploration of boundaries. Neither revealed too much, neither backed down, each acknowledging the other's power.

Wulfstan didn't take her bait. Instead, he closed his eyes and bowed, a slight smile still lingering on his lips. 'I'm sure we will have ample time to discuss your past and future adventures,' he said. 'But for now, I will leave you to get familiar with your new home.'

As Wulfstan left her, Gunnhild glanced around the room, the enormity of her situation slowly sinking in. Here she was, a queen in a foreign land, surrounded by unfamiliar sights and sounds. But she had faced hardships before, and she decided that adapting to her new home would be another challenge she was ready to meet.

A familiar face drew her attention.

'Astrid,' Gunnhild exclaimed, a genuine smile adorning her face. 'My heart warms at the sight of you!'

'Welcome, my queen,' Astrid responded politely. 'I have prepared your chambers for you. Do you want to see them?'

'I would like nothing better!' Gunnhild replied, casting a brief glance and a playful smile at Eirik.

Astrid led Gunnhild through a set of ornate doors to a

private corridor. Walking along, they passed various rooms until they reached an elegantly carved wooden door. Astrid pushed it open with a gesture of welcome.

The chamber was an impressive sight. The outer room served as a private sitting area, with a plush, richly embroidered bench and two carved wooden chairs around a low table. The table bore a simple arrangement of wildflowers. Beside the sitting area was a hearth, and on the floor lay a woven rug with a pattern of intertwining Norse symbols. Gunnhild could imagine herself huddled there during cold winter evenings, the fire crackling and warming the room.

Leading on from this was the bedchamber. A large, intricately carved bed dominated the room. The beddings were layered with warm furs and embroidered linen, and on the bed lay her favourite cloak, which Astrid had carefully packed for the journey. Tapestries hung on the walls, depicting familiar scenes from the battles of Sigurd Hjort and Harald Fairhair.

Next to the bed was a wooden dressing table, atop which sat a bronze mirror. Various combs, brooches and hairpins, the tools of Astrid's trade, were neatly arranged on its surface.

'It's beautiful, Astrid,' Gunnhild said, her voice tinged with gratitude. 'It feels like a piece of our homeland. Thank you.'

Astrid beamed with pleasure, her eyes glinting with satisfaction. 'I'm glad you approve, my queen.'

Gunnhild immediately felt at ease in this corner of the palace, a place of her own where she could go to gather her strength. She would get used to this place. She would learn its customs, its people. She would become a part of it. And in time, perhaps, they would accept her as one of their own.

CHAPTER: SHIPWRECKED

Arinbjørn was on the verge of drifting into sleep when he was abruptly awakened by the sound of someone pounding on the gates of his Jórvik estate.

'Open this gate!' an angry voice demanded.

Arinbjørn hastily sprang out of bed, quickly fastening his sword belt around his waist as he dashed through the darkened and empty common room. Stepping into the courtyard, he found five of his hirdmen, just as ill-prepared as he was, already drenched by the relentless rain that greeted them outside.

'Are we under attack?' Arinbjørn inquired of young Torfinn Einarsson, son of Jarl Torv-Einar of the Orkneys.

'No, my lord,' Torfinn replied. 'However, five men stand outside our gates, four of them armed.'

'Open the gate and prepare to defend against any potential intruders,' Arinbjørn commanded.

Within moments, the gate swung open, allowing a group of rain-soaked figures to enter. Among them were four guards, alongside a burly man with a concealed face beneath a clinging hood, his hands tightly bound.

'Lord Arinbjørn,' said one of the guards, 'this man approached the city gates after nightfall, insisting on gaining entry. He refused to disclose his name but claims to be responding to your invitation.'

'Is that so?' Comprehension of the situation dawned upon

Arinbjørn. 'Perhaps, if he removes his hood, I may ascertain his identity and verify the validity of his claims.'

One of the guards pulled back the stranger's hood, while another held a flickering torch just a foot from his face.

'Ah, as I suspected,' Arinbjørn remarked. 'He speaks the truth, although I had not anticipated his arrival amid this weather and darkness. I am grateful for your escorting him to my abode.'

The four guards departed, leaving the uninvited guest in the custody of Arinbjørn without further discussion.

'My sword, please,' the stranger requested, his hands still bound.

One of the guards handed a sheathed sword to Torfinn before departing through the gate.

Arinbjørn waited until the gate closed before he spoke again.

'Welcome, Egil Skallagrimsson. It has been quite some time since our last encounter. I fear this meeting may be our last unless you depart as discreetly as you arrived before dawn. King Eirik would have you killed on sight, and his city boasts a legion of loyal troops.'

'How your hospitality has soured, Arinbjørn,' Egil retorted. 'Yet, I would not have ventured here unless it were absolutely necessary. Might we continue this discussion within? I have endured two days and nights of rain and wind, and there is nothing I desire more than to sit by the fireplace, clad in dry clothes against my skin.'

Egil extended his bound hands. Arinbjørn drew his sword to sever the ropes before they proceeded together to the common room.

'Torfinn,' Arinbjørn instructed, 'awaken Borr and inform him of our guest this night.'

Before long, they found themselves savouring a mug of ale

by the fireplace. Egil, wrapped in three woollen blankets, allowed his damp clothes to hang and dry. Taking a generous bite of the bread served to him, he drew his chair closer to the crackling flames.

'Why have you come?' Arinbjørn queried, unable to conceal his frustration at once again being forced to choose between his friend and his loyalty to his lord. 'Surely you are aware that by entering a city under the rule of Eirik and Gunnhild, your days are numbered?'

'Not by choice,' Egil mumbled, mouth full of bread. After chewing and swallowing, he continued, 'I was on my way to visit King Aethelstan when the storm forced us to disembark at the Humber. I lost two men, and our ship is beyond repair. In a desperate situation, I left my crew with the ship and entrusted our lives to my old friend Arinbjørn.'

'You push the boundaries of our friendship, Egil. I cannot aid you without invoking the wrath of Eirik and Gunnhild, and you know this,' Arinbjørn stated firmly.

'I understand, and I apologise,' Egil responded. 'However, in the past, you have spoken on my behalf and managed to keep your own head intact.'

'That was before you slew Ragnvald and raised the nithing pole against the King and Queen of Norway,' Arinbjørn reminded him.

'They left me with no choice!' Egil exclaimed.

'And now, you have left me with no choice,' Arinbjørn said. 'Eirik will soon learn of your presence in his city.'

Egil nodded, taking another bite of the bread.

'Very well,' Arinbjørn declared, rising from his seat. 'Put on your damp clothes once more. We shall meet with King Eirik in his great hall.'

CHAPTER: MERCY

Through the pouring rain, Arinbjørn and Egil trudged the short distance towards Eirik's great hall with an escort of ten armed hirdmen.

'When we arrive,' Arinbjørn advised, 'you must humble yourself before the king. Kneel and clasp his foot, and I shall speak on your behalf.'

Egil offered no reply.

Arinbjørn announced their presence to the guards stationed outside the door, and moments later, they stood before King Eirik, who was seated at a table near the fireplace.

'Arinbjørn, my friend,' Eirik inquired, 'what brings you here after nightfall, accompanied by armed men?'

A tense pause hung in the air, as many of Eirik's and Arinbjørn's men instinctively rested their hands on their sword hilts.

'My apologies, my lord, for our late arrival and armed entourage,' began Arinbjørn. 'I bring before you a man who has travelled from distant lands seeking reconciliation. It is a great honour when your adversaries, aware of the extent of your wrath, voluntarily journey to your doorstep. Show this man your grace and mercy, for he has magnified your honour by braving treacherous seas and dangers to find you.'

Arinbjørn bowed low, allowing Eirik to cast his gaze over his shoulder at the man standing behind him. Closing his eyes, Arinbjørn awaited the response, which came with unexpected restraint.

'How dare you stand before me, Egil? Our previous encounter would leave you with no hope of surviving such a confrontation,' Eirik challenged.

Without uttering a word, Egil stepped forward and knelt before Eirik, clasping his foot. Then, he sang:

'With crosswinds far cruising
I came on my wave-horse,
Eirik, England's warder
Eager soon to see.
Now wielder of wound-flash,
Wight dauntless in daring,
That strong strand of Harald's
Stout lineage I meet.'

Eirik took a step back, freeing his foot from the Icelander's grasp. 'I need not enumerate your crimes, for they are countless and abhorrent, each one deserving of denying you leave from this hall alive. You can expect nothing from me except imminent death,' Eirik declared.

A sudden gasp reverberated through the room as Gunnhild entered through a side door, her eyes blazing with fury.

'Surely, you will slay him at once?' Gunnhild hissed, her voice filled with intense anger. 'Remember, my lord king, that Egil has brought death upon your son and your friends! He has even cursed you, your kin, and your lands. The gods demand that he pay for his despicable deeds with his life.'

Her words carried an unmistakable weight, emphasising the depth of Gunnhild's rage and her unwavering determination for retribution.

'The king should not be tempted to have Egil slain under the cover of night, for such an act would be murder,' Arinbjørn interjected, his voice steady and resolute.

Gunnhild's eyes narrowed with an intense glare as Arinbjørn challenged Eirik's potential course of action. Her grip tightened around the edge of her gown, revealing her deep-rooted opposition to Arinbjørn's words.

Eirik turned his gaze towards Gunnhild, his eyes meeting hers in a silent exchange of understanding and unspoken tension. The weight of the decision hung heavily in the air as Eirik contemplated the consequences.

Finally, Eirik turned back to Arinbjørn and delivered his response, his voice filled with a mix of authority and measured restraint. 'So be it, Arinbjørn. Egil shall be allowed to live through this night. Take him back to your dwelling and bring him to me in the morning to face his judgment.'

A flicker of triumph gleamed in Gunnhild's eyes as Eirik made his decision. She stood tall, her posture exuding an air of vindication and satisfaction.

Arinbjørn bowed once more, acknowledging Eirik's command while subtly trying to bridge the gap between Gunnhild's vehement opposition and the potential for reconciliation. 'Thank you, my lord. It is my fervent hope that your relationship with Egil may take a more favourable turn. Though he has undoubtedly committed severe crimes against you, it is crucial to acknowledge the hardships he has endured at the hands of your kin. Your father's actions, driven by the slander of wicked men, resulted in the exile of Egil's family. And even you, for the sake of Berg-Onund, broke our laws and branded him an outlaw. Egil is a man who will not tolerate injustice or disregard any slight. In every case brought before judgment, one must undertake a thorough examination of both the act and its underlying reasons. I shall take my leave now and ensure Egil remains under my watch for the night.'

Gunnhild felt a mix of frustration and indignation as Arinbjørn appealed to Eirik's sense of fairness and understanding. Her fingers curled into tight fists as she struggled to contain her seething emotions.

Upon their return to the estate, Arinbjørn led Egil to a

small room in the loft.

'Eirik was indeed wrathful, as expected, but I sensed a slight softening of his demeanour towards the end. However, Gunnhild will devote all her energy to thwarting your cause. My advice is to spend the night composing a poem of praise for King Eirik, which you can recite when you stand before him tomorrow. With luck, you may keep your head and even find reconciliation,' Arinbjørn suggested.

Egil sighed. 'I shall try, but the last thing I desire is to sing King Eirik's praises.'

'Nevertheless, give it a try, for it may well be the last thing you ever do,' Arinbjørn warned.

Arinbjørn departed but returned after midnight, bearing food and drink to sustain Egil through the night. Egil wore a look of misery.

'How are you faring?' Arinbjørn inquired.

Egil shook his head slowly.

'Have you managed to compose any verses?' Arinbjørn asked.

'No, just fragments and snippets,' Egil admitted.

'Why?' Arinbjørn questioned.

Egil gestured towards the window at the far end of the room.

'The swallow?' Arinbjørn guessed.

'Yes. It has perched there, incessantly twittering,' Egil confirmed.

'Why didn't you simply chase it away?' Arinbjørn asked.

'I did,' Egil answered.

'And?' Arinbjørn pressed.

'It returned. Every time,' Egil revealed.

Arinbjørn made his way towards the swallow, which observed him with one eye as he approached. Only when he was two steps away did it take flight. Arinbjørn watched as it soared directly towards Eirik's great hall. In the dim light, the bird seemed to grow in size, resembling a winged shadow. Before vanishing from sight, it was nearly the size of a person. Or rather, the size of a woman.

'Gunnhild,' Arinbjørn muttered.

'Perhaps,' Egil agreed.

Arinbjørn nodded. 'Very well. I shall remain here until you finish. If the unnatural bird returns, I shall fetch my bow.'

'Thank you, my friend,' Egil said gratefully.

CHAPTER: HEAD-RANSOM

The next morning, Arinbjørn and Egil, accompanied by sixteen armed housecarls, made their way into King Eirik's grand hall. Arinbjørn positioned half of the escort outside, under the command of Torfinn Einarsson, while the remaining guards followed him inside.

'Why do you bring an army to my home, Arinbjørn?' Eirik asked, his tone laced with curiosity and perhaps a hint of concern.

Arinbjørn's gaze swept across the crowded hall, acutely aware of their being outnumbered. With utmost respect, he addressed the king, seeking a peaceful resolution.

'My king, I have returned with Egil Skallagrimsson, who willingly remained under my protection throughout the night. I beseech you to consider reconciliation and grant him a chance to depart on amicable terms. In both my words and actions, I have always sought to honour you. I have forsaken all my lands, possessions, kinsmen and friends in Norway to follow your cause, when others abandoned it. You have been a benevolent lord to me. I implore you to pass judgment in a manner that does not sever the strong bond between us.'

Gunnhild, unable to contain her disapproval, interjected sharply, her voice cutting through the air. 'Enough, Arinbjørn! You have rendered great services to King Eirik, and your loyalty has been duly rewarded. Your indebtedness lies more with King Eirik than with Egil. It is not your place to demand impunity for

Egil, fully aware of the crimes he has committed.'

Arinbjørn's gaze shifted from Gunnhild to Eirik, seeking a favourable response from the king. Eirik remained silent, his inclination often veering towards reticence when faced with difficult decisions.

'Should you and Gunnhild already be resolved in your stance against reconciling with Egil,' Arinbjørn continued, his voice steady and resolute, 'it would be honourable to grant him respite and allow him to depart without persecution. He came here of his own volition, seeking peace.'

Once again, Eirik maintained his silence, leaving the weight of the decision hanging in the air.

'By your words and actions, you are more faithful to Egil than to King Eirik,' Gunnhild said with unwavering determination. 'If Egil rides from here today, he will be with King Aethelstan within a week. And Eirik will appear like the weakest of kings, unable to avenge the evil crimes against himself and his kin.'

'Nobody will call Eirik a great king for slaying a landholder who has freely come into his power,' Arinbjørn said. 'But if my lord desires to achieve greatness by slaying this Icelander, then we will make this deed worthy of record.'

'What do you mean?' Eirik asked.

'I mean, my lord, that you can take Egil's life when we all lay dead in your hall, my followers and I. Far better treatment would I have expected of you, than preferring to see me dead on the ground rather than allowing me to spare one man's life.'

Eirik rose. 'You are a wondrous champion, Arinbjørn, for you would rather give your own life than see your friend be slain. I would loathe to harm you if it came to this. But the charges against Egil Skallagrimsson are sufficient to justify any judgment I pass on him.'

Arinbjørn swallowed and looked around the hall once more, running out of options. He had failed in talking himself out of this vice, and he could not hope to fight his way out.

He felt a hand on his shoulder and turned to find Egil standing beside him.

'Thank you, my brother,' Egil whispered.

The hall fell silent as Egil, standing beside Arinbjørn, drew a deep breath and began reciting his poem with a commanding voice.

'Westward I sailed the wave,
Within me Odin gave
The sea of song I bear.
So it is my wont to fare.
I launched my floating oak.
When loosening ice floes broke,
My mind a galleon fraught
With load of minstrel thought.'

Arinbjørn cast a quick glance at Gunnhild, half-expecting her to interrupt Egil's impending recital. To his surprise, she appeared as captivated as the rest of the audience, engrossed in the unfolding events.

'A prince doth hold me guest,
Praise be his due confessed:
Of Odin's mead let draught
In England now be quaffed.
Laud bear I to the king,
Loudly his honour sing;
Silence I crave around,
My song of praise is found.

'Sire, mark the tale I tell,
Such heed beseems thee well;
Better I chaunt my strain,
If stillness hushed I gain.
The monarch's wars in word
Widely have peoples heard,

But Odin saw alone
Bodies before him strown.'

Eirik sat upright, his gaze fixed keenly on Egil, listening intently to each verse. Gunnhild, despite her reservations, was also caught up in the enchantment of Egil's recitation.

'Spears crossing dashed,
Sword-edges clashed:
Glory and fame
Gat Eirik's name.

'Monarch, at thy will
Judge my minstrel skill:
Silence thus to find
Sweetly cheered my mind.'

Verse after verse, Egil continued, weaving a mesmerising tale that resonated with every soul present. Arinbjørn watched, his eyes shifting between Eirik and Gunnhild, astonished by the effect of Egil's words, leaving every man and woman in the hall spellbound.

'Moved my mouth with word
From my heart's ground stirred,
Draught of Odin's wave
Due to warrior brave.

'Silence I have broken,
A sovereign's glory spoken:
Words I knew well-fitting
Warrior-council sitting.
Praise from heart I bring,
Praise to honoured king:
Plain I sang and clear
Song that all could hear.'

When Egil finally concluded his poem, he kneeled before King Eirik, awaiting his judgment. The room held its breath, the tension palpable.

'Well recited was the poem,' Eirik said, his voice carrying a blend of admiration and sternness. 'Arinbjørn, I have reached a decision in this matter. Your impassioned defence of Egil's cause, your willingness to risk conflict for his sake, has not gone unnoticed. For your sake, I shall allow Egil to depart from my lands unharmed and safe.'

Eirik rose from his throne and approached Egil with measured steps. His voice resonated with a blend of caution and finality. 'Egil Skallagrimsson, you may keep your head upon your shoulders, but be aware that once you leave my presence and this hall, you shall never cross paths with me, my sons, or my people again. Reconciliation with me or my kin seeking vengeance is an impossibility.'

Eirik returned to his throne, a sense of resolution radiating from him.

Arinbjørn bowed deeply to Eirik, then to Gunnhild, before he turned and walked out of the great hall with Egil and his housecarls.

Neither spoke until they were alone at Arinbjørn's estate.

'I regret that I cannot provide you with a team of shipwrights and carpenters to repair your vessel before winter,' Arinbjørn said. 'However, I can offer you the assistance of fifty armed men who will safely escort you and your crew to King Aethelstan's realm, where you will be welcomed with open arms.'

Egil's expression softened, his appreciation evident in his eyes. 'Thank you, my most daring and loyal friend.' He removed two massive gold rings from his arms and extended them to Arinbjørn. 'These were bestowed upon me by King Aethelstan after the battle at Vinheath, where Torolv fell.'

Arinbjørn accepted the rings with gratitude and acknowledged the significance of the gift. 'Thank you, Egil. I, too, have something for you.'

Arinbjørn left Egil in the common room, but swiftly returned with a sword in his hands. He presented it to Egil with reverence. 'This is Dragvandill, a sword that has passed through the hands of your father, Skallagrim, and your uncle, Torolv Kveldulfsson. It is a blade of unparalleled power and a testament to their legacy. No man has ever been defeated while wielding this sword.'

CHAPTER: KING EDMUND

Jórvik, 939

'All hail King Edmund!' the herald proclaimed, filling King Eirik's grand hall with anticipation. Every man present stood at attention as the young monarch, Edmund, son of Edward, made his entrance accompanied by his retinue.

'He's just a boy, no more than twenty winters,' Gunnhild whispered.

'He may be young, but he is the king nonetheless,' Eirik replied softly. 'We must play our parts in this charade.'

As the young king approached King Eirik and Queen Gunnhild, Eirik knelt before him. Gunnhild winced, following suit, and awaited the command to rise. However, instead of the anticipated instruction, Edmund spoke with authority.

'Eric Haraldsson, you have served as the king's representative in Eoforwic and Northumbria. Now, my brother Aethelstan has passed away, and your service to the king of England is no longer required.'

Eirik and Gunnhild exchanged bewildered glances, their confusion palpable. Eirik mustered the courage to speak, seeking clarification from the young king.

'But, my lord,' Eirik began, still kneeling, 'as I've been a loyal underking to King Aethelstan, would it not be in our best interests to renew our alliance rather than dissolve it?'

Edmund's response was swift and uncompromising. 'You were never an ally of my brother. You were his servant, albeit a competent one. However, I prefer to have individuals of my own choosing in key positions within my realm.' As an afterthought, he added, 'You may rise.'

Eirik rose and bowed respectfully. 'May I ask who will rule Jórvik in your name?'

'Olaf Guthfrithson will be my jarl in Eoforwic,' Edmund said.

Gunnhild, unable to contain her shock, gasped involuntarily, hastily disguising it as a cough. The mention of Olaf Guthfrithson, the infamous Viking king of Dublin, had caught her off guard.

'As you wish, my king,' Eirik said. 'Yet, I must raise a concern. Olaf Guthfrithson, whom you have chosen to rule Jórvik in your name, was allied with the kings of Scotland and Strathclyde against Wessex. He fought against your brother at Brunanburh. Olaf is not a friend of the heirs of King Alfred.'

Edmund's voice carried an air of conviction. 'I am not my brother! Olaf is a direct descendant of Ivar the Boneless, and his claim to Eoforwic is legitimate. He has repented, and we have reached an agreement that is mutually beneficial. His presence will bring peace to the North.'

Eirik bowed once again. 'As you wish, my king.'

Edmund's attention shifted, turning to another matter. 'I understand that your daughter is married to Erlend Einarsson, son of the Jarl of Orkney?'

'She is,' Eirik replied.

'Excellent,' Edmund remarked with a hint of satisfaction. 'I am sure you will be welcome there. Shall we say, in three days' time?'

CHAPTER: KING EIRIK

Orkney, 947

'Wulfstan!' Eirik called out as the aged man disembarked from the ship. 'Eight winters have passed since I last saw you in Jórvik. What brings you to these shores?'

'Necessity, my lord,' Wulfstan replied, offering a respectful bow to Gunnhild. 'My lady,' the archbishop added.

'Please,' Gunnhild said warmly, 'join us in the great hall and share your troubles.'

'Thank you for your hospitality,' Wulfstan said gratefully, casting his gaze around the surroundings. 'You seem to have prospered, Eric. Your ships, your men, your new buildings and splendid attire.'

'Life becomes easier when one is free to travel, raid, and trade at will,' Eirik replied.

'Ah, yes. We have heard much of the ventures of Eric Bloodaxe since you departed our lands,' Wulfstan remarked with a hint of jest.

'Perhaps you should join us?' Eirik suggested.

Wulfstan chuckled heartily. 'Alas! My lord does not permit me to embark on Viking exploits. He has other plans in store for me.'

'Such as?' Eirik inquired.

'Saving Northumbria from King Eadred,' Wulfstan disclosed.

'Another king of England,' Eirik acknowledged.

'Yes, the third of Edward's sons. Even more callous than his brother, Edmund,' Wulfstan shared, concern shadowing his expression.

'We have much to discuss,' Gunnhild interjected. 'But first, join us inside and share a meal. There will be time to delve into the details.'

'Thank you,' Wulfstan expressed his appreciation as they entered Eirik's longhouse, a structure of impressive stature, its interior smelling of smoked wood and roasted meat. The crackling fireplace near the far end provided a welcoming warmth against the chill of the outside.

'Now, you may remember my sons,' Eirik gestured towards the young men seated at the nearest table. 'Gamle, Guttorm, Harald, and Ragnfrød.'

Wulfstan approached the table, offering greetings to each of the young men in turn.

'And where are your other children?' the archbishop inquired as he settled into a comfortable chair near the crackling fireplace.

'Our daughter, Ragnhild, is married to the Erlend Einarsson of Orkney. They reside on the island just north of here. Our youngest sons, Erling, Gudrød, and Sigurd, are currently fostered by Harald Bluetooth of Denmark,' Eirik revealed.

'A shrewd move,' Wulfstan acknowledged. 'An alliance with Denmark could prove advantageous for the heirs of Harald Fairhair.'

'It may indeed,' Gunnhild responded. 'But please, enlighten us about the situation in Northumbria.'

A heavy sigh escaped Wulfstan's lips. 'As I'm sure you know, King Edmund lost his patience with Olaf Guthricson and had him removed. After his brother's demise, Eadred sought to install another ruler of Dublin, the ruthless Olaf Sithricson, as the jarl of Northumbria. When we resisted, Eadred responded with brutal reprisals, burning villages and executing the populace. While we can defend Eoforwic, we cannot safeguard the entirety of Northumbria. We are faced with the grim choice of accepting another Olaf of Dublin as our ruler or enduring relentless massacres of our people.'

'And you seek my counsel on this matter?' Eirik queried.

'No,' Wulfstan corrected, his voice solemn, eyes intent on Eirik, 'we seek you to be our king.'

The room fell quiet, until Eirik booming laughter echoed broke the silence, his eyes twinkling with amusement. 'I have already attempted that.'

'Indeed, but that was as Aethelstan's underking. Now, we implore you to become the king of an independent Northumbria,' Wulfstan proposed.

'And spend my days battling Eadred's armies? Why should I do that?' Eirik questioned.

'Because Northumbria has the potential to become a formidable kingdom, boasting plentiful resources and a substantial Norse population. It is precisely what you need to reclaim the title of king of Norway, for yourself or your sons,' Wulfstan replied, laying out the enticing prospects.

Gunnhild's hand gently rested on Eirik's arm, offering support. 'Do you speak on behalf of the city of Jórvik?' she asked.

'I do,' Wulfstan confirmed.

'And what about the church?' Eirik inquired.

'Yes,' Wulfstan responded, 'but naturally, you will need to be baptised once more.'

'Again?' Eirik feigned surprise.

'Yes,' Wulfstan affirmed.

'And then, I must vanquish Eadred?' Eirik sought further clarification.

'Yes, and likely Olaf Sithricson as well,' Wulfstan revealed.

Eirik nodded slowly, the weight of the moment apparently

sinking in, until a faint smile graced his face. 'I accept. Prepare the great hall of Jórvik for my triumphant return.'

CHAPTER: HOWDEN

Following the council at Jórvik, Eirik, Gunnhild and Arinbjørn, with an escort of a hundred men, set out for the village of Howden. Two days had passed since Eadred's forces had attacked, and Gunnhild apprehension grew as she looked to the south.

As they crested the final hill, the extent of the destruction was laid bare before them. Howden, once a thriving settlement, now lay in ruin. Thatched-roof cottages were reduced to skeletal remains, charred wood and scorched stone. Gardens, once a source of sustenance, were trampled and stripped bare. The village square was deserted, the market stalls destroyed. Farm animals lay lifeless in the fields, their bodies stark against the battered landscape. The verdant green of the land was marred by the burnt, blackened scars of fire.

The local Christ church, a simple wooden structure with a high cross at its apex, had suffered, too. Its roof was collapsed, the sturdy oak doors were broken, and pieces of the glass windows lay scattered on the scorched earth.

As they moved deeper into the village, the evidence of Eadred's wrath was stark. The village well had been filled in, the heavy stone capping it pushed aside and replaced with debris. The granary, once filled with the community's stored food, was now a burnt shell, its contents reduced to blackened cinders.

Survivors of the massacre were scattered among the ruins, trying to save what they could. Some were nursing injuries, others were aimlessly wandering amid the wreckage of their lives, their faces hollow. The air was heavy with the scent of smoke and an overwhelming sense of loss. The silence was broken only by the occasional whimpers of children and the low murmurs of the despairing adults.

Nearby, Gunnhild noticed a young woman, her eyes wide and glazed, cradling an infant. The remnants of their home smouldered behind them, the flames having consumed their possessions. Gunnhild approached, her heart heavy with shared sorrow. 'We're here to help,' she assured them.

The woman looked up, her eyes brimming with a complex mix of fear, grief and a glimmer of relief. 'They came in the night ...,' she choked out, tears streaming down her dirty face.

Eirik dismounted his horse. 'This was more than a simple raid ... This was a statement,' he murmured through gritted teeth. 'This place yielded no plunder and no strategic advantage. It was a warning, a demonstration of Eadred's might.'

Arinbjørn, his voice hard and resolute, suggested, 'We need to retaliate and show Eadred that we won't stand for this.'

Eirik, his gaze still lingering on the ruins, replied, 'And invite more destruction? First, we ensure the safety of our people.'

'We need to establish a military presence to deter any further attacks,' Arinbjørn said.

Eirik frowned. 'How do you suggest we do that? There are hundreds of villages like this, with no palisades or fortifications.'

Arinbjørn nodded. 'Advanced sentries might not prevent an attack, but we can ensure immediate retaliation and aid to affected areas.'

Eirik straightened and issued an order to his men. 'There is work to do! Start with the well and remove those carcasses!'

Eirik turned towards Arinbjørn. 'Reinforce our southern garrisons. I want patrols on the roads day and night. The people need to see our presence, feel our protection.'

Arinbjørn responded with a curt nod, his expression

resolute. 'Understood, my lord. It shall be done.'

CHAPTER: COUNCIL

The air in the grand hall of Jórvik was thick with tension as Gunnhild settled into the sturdy wooden chair at the long table. Eirik had convened an emergency council after the arrivals of ealdormen Aelfric of Loidis and Oswulf of Bebbanburgh. Maps of Northumbria stretched across the broad wooden table, punctuated with tankards of mead.

'Speak, Aelfric. What's going on in Loidis?' Eirik's voice sliced through the quiet.

Aelfric didn't mince words. 'It's a mess, Eirik. Eadred's men come in like a storm, wreak havoc, and are gone before we can even pull our boots on. They hit Howden last night... Took nothing. Not a coin, not a sheep. They're just flexing their muscles.'

Arinbjørn slammed his fist on to the table. 'We can't sit back. This is a dare we can't ignore.'

'We need to respond, but we can't rush into a war unprepared,' Eirik warned, studying the map. 'And you, Oswulf? What's the news from Bebbanburgh? Trouble in the north?'

Oswulf, a brute of a man with a beard as untamed as his northern lands, shook his head. 'The men of Alba are buzzing, but it's the same old. We got it under control. It's Eadred we need to worry about.'

King Eirik nodded and looked around at the council. 'Very well. I trust you to secure our northern regions while we respond to the challenge in the south.'

As they discussed their plans, Gunnhild felt a knot of

worry in her stomach. Was this how it would be? A constant battle for power and control?

Wulfstan's voice brought her back to the conversation. 'My king, if I might?'

'Yes, Wulfstan?' Eirik replied, looking up from the map.

'Eadred's strategy could be an attempt to undermine your authority, to portray you as an incapable protector.'

A few heads bobbed in agreement.

'A valid point,' Gunnhild acknowledged. 'We must respond swiftly and decisively. We cannot have our people living in fear. They need to know that their king and queen will protect them. I suggest we visit Howden on the morrow.'

CHAPTER: RIPON

Jórvik, Northumbria, 948

Eirik placed a round piece of metal on the table and pushed it towards Gunnhild. She picked it up, examining the small, silver coin adorned with a crude image of a sword and the inscription 'Eric Rex' on one side. Before she could turn it over, the doors to the great hall in Jórvik swung open, and Archbishop Wulfstan burst in, accompanied by a monk and two flustered guards.

Apologies were quickly offered by one of the guards. 'He would not wait, and we were hesitant to restrain him by force.'

Eirik stood, acknowledging the guards before turning his attention to Wulfstan. 'What is the matter, Archbishop?'

Wulfstan's expression was grave as he relayed the news. 'There has been another assault, my lord.'

Eirik's brow furrowed. 'Where?'

'Ripon, a day's ride northwest of here,' Wulfstan replied.

Curiosity mingled with concern, Eirik pressed further. 'Tell me what transpired.'

Wulfstan turned to the young monk by his side. 'Durwin here witnessed the events first-hand. He can provide you with an account of what occurred.'

Durwin swallowed nervously before addressing the king. 'My lord, as I was preparing to leave Ripon at noon, I heard the sound of riders approaching from the south. I turned and saw more than fifty soldiers. Moments later, I heard screams, and I took cover in some nearby bushes, watching the scene unfold.'

Gunnhild, rising from her seat, poured the monk a cup of wine and handed it to him. 'Please, take this. It may help steady your nerves.'

'Thank you, my lady,' Durwin said, accepting the offering and taking a few sips before continuing his account.

'A group of soldiers on foot accompanied the riders. From my hiding place, I could not discern their exact numbers, but I estimate there were around a hundred men donned in chain mail.'

Eirik interjected, questioning the monk's identification. 'You refer to them as soldiers. How can you be certain they were not brigands or the hirdmen of a jarl?'

'They all wore similar chain mail armour and helmets, my lord,' Durwin replied with conviction.

Eirik turned to Wulfstan for confirmation. 'Are these King Eadred's men? Have they ventured as far north as Ripon?'

Wulfstan nodded solemnly. 'Indeed, my lord. I fear it was no coincidence that they chose to attack there. Please allow Durwin to finish his account.'

Durwin wiped his mouth, composed himself, and continued. 'The soldiers spread throughout the town, pillaging homes and ruthlessly slaying anyone who stood in their way. Fires erupted, and countless terrified souls ran past my hiding place as they desperately sought to escape.'

'Were they pursued?' Eirik inquired further.

'No, my lord. The soldiers allowed them to flee. Instead, a sizable force surrounded the cathedral and set it ablaze,' Durwin replied, his voice filled with anguish.

Eirik furrowed his brow, his gaze shifting to Wulfstan. 'Why would they burn a cathedral? King Eadred is a Christian ruler.'

Wulfstan's expression revealed a bitter truth. 'To spite me,

I'm afraid.'

'You? What have you done to incur such a reaction from Eadred?'

'I pledged my loyalty to him after the death of King Edmund,' Wulfstan confessed. 'However, my faith in young Eadred proved misplaced.'

'Eadred is a vindictive man,' Eirik observed. 'Do you believe he is here with his army?'

Wulfstan nodded solemnly. 'I assume so, my lord. Eadred rarely misses an opportunity to exact his vengeance upon the people.'

Eirik rose from his seat, a glimmer of excitement flickering in his eyes. Gunnhild, intimately acquainted with the fiery spirit that dwelled within her husband, immediately recognised the familiar look of anticipation that danced in his gaze. It was a gleam that often presaged the call to action, igniting the core of his warrior's heart and infusing him with an unyielding resolve.

In these moments, Gunnhild could not help but marvel at the unquenchable fire that burned within Eirik. His warrior spirit blazed with an intensity that seemed to grow even stronger in the face of adversity, ready to confront any obstacle that dared to threaten their rule.

With a voice brimming with conviction, Eirik declared, 'Very well. He must learn to stay out of Northumbria. We shall dispatch scouts and prepare our army for battle.'

CHAPTER: FOREBODING

'Be careful, my love.' Gunnhild's voice trembled with concern, her eyes filled with an unsettling mixture of love and foreboding.

Eirik paused in his preparations, his hand hovering over his belt as he turned to face her. 'What troubles you, Gunnhild? Your concern is unlike any I have witnessed before. What have you seen in your visions?'

'A shallow river. And flames that engulf everything in their path.'

Eirik's brows furrowed. 'Have you seen my death in these visions?'

Gunnhild's gaze met his. 'Many times, my love.'

A flicker of wry humour danced in Eirik's eyes as he responded. 'In battle, I hope?'

A gentle smile graced Gunnhild's lips as she reassured him. 'Of course. In the heat of the fray, where you belong.'

Eirik chuckled. 'Well, I am not growing any younger, and my time will come. But tell me, my love, do you know what course of action to take should fate deem it so?'

Gunnhild's voice held steadfast determination as she replied. 'We shall seek refuge on the Orkneys until our sons are ready to claim the throne of Norway.'

Eirik leaned down to kiss her, but Gunnhild soon pulled away, her mind remained consumed by worry.

'Which of our sons will join you in this battle?' she inquired, her tone tinged with apprehension.

'Gamle, Guttorm and Harald, they are all skilled fighters. Ragnfrød, though old enough, bears the burden of an injured shoulder.'

Gunnhild nodded, her unease refusing to dissipate. She retrieved a roll of cloth from the table and gently placed it in Eirik's hands. As he unwrapped it, his gaze fell upon the barbed arrow nestled within, its menacing design capturing his attention.

Eirik examined the *flein*, its shaft carefully balanced and its barbed head capable of piercing even the toughest chain mail. A wry smile played upon his lips.

'This is a wicked arrow, crafted with precision,' he murmured. 'Its narrow head allows it to penetrate even the strongest armour, while the barbs ensure its extraction will inflict further harm.'

Gunnhild's voice resonated with a hint of suggestion as she spoke. 'For Eadred, perhaps?'

Eirik's response was swift. He gently wrapped the arrow in the cloth and returned it to her grasp. 'No, not for Eadred. There will always be another offspring of Alfred's ready to ascend the throne.'

Gunnhild nodded, understanding his intentions.

'Save it for Haakon,' Eirik declared, his voice firm with determination.

'I will,' Gunnhild affirmed, her voice laced with a mix of hope and desperation. 'But please, my love, return to me.'

Eirik smiled. 'I shall do my utmost to return. But if I do not, heed my words. Leave this place immediately. Do not spend another night in Jórvik once I have fallen.'

CHAPTER: CASTLEFORD

'Stay low and remain silent,' Arinbjørn whispered, his voice barely audible.

Instead of engaging in a direct confrontation with King Eadred on the open battlefield, Eirik had chosen a different strategy. He had led his army to Castleford, situated southeast of Loidis, where the ancient Roman road intersected with the River Aire. Concealed on the northern bank, Eirik's forces lay in wait, their eyes fixed on the approaching Saxon soldiers marching in a narrow formation.

As the cavalry ventured into the ford, the water reached the bellies of their horses. Arinbjørn's gaze narrowed upon spotting King Eadred and his personal guard approaching the river.

Without a word, Arinbjørn nudged Eirik with his elbow and pointed towards the river. Three heartbeats later, Eirik nodded in confirmation. Raising his arm, he signalled his warriors, and a rustling of anticipation swept through the hidden forces as weapons were brandished. The anticipation was palpable, like the calm before a storm.

When King Eadred and his guard reached the middle of the river, Eirik lowered his arm and Harald Eiriksson shouted, 'Now! Attack!'

The command reverberated through the ranks, unleashing the full force of Eirik's battle-hardened army. With a resounding roar, the hidden warriors burst forth from their concealed positions, charging with Harald leading the way, closely followed by Eirik and Arinbjørn.

'Arnkel!' Eirik's voice boomed. 'The archers!'

To their left, Arnkel Einarsson, the youngest son of the Jarl of Orkney, led a group of warriors to silence the enemy archers before they could ready their bows to rain deadly arrows upon Eirik's forces.

The Saxons, taken aback by the unexpected assault, struggled to organise a coherent defence. King Eadred and parts of the cavalry struggled to turn their horses and return to the northern bank, while the foot soldiers drew their weapons and hastened to assume a defensive formation.

All semblance of organisation was lost when war cries sounded from the east side of the road as well. Gamle and Guttorm Eiriksson led the other half of Eirik's army in a ferocious attack on the rear of the beleaguered Saxons. In a masterful stroke of coordination, Torfinn Einarsson emerged from the north. His mounted warriors charged forth, sealing the fate of Eadred's infantry.

However, King Eadred and his cavalry made no attempt to join the battle unfolding on the north bank. Instead, they were forced to bear witness as Eirik's army mercilessly struck down the Saxons. Hindered by the river, the riders were unable to charge at full speed, and any who attempted to cross were swiftly dispatched before they could reach the safety of the opposite bank.

'Eadred escapes,' Arinbjørn observed, his voice laced with a mix of disappointment and resignation.

On the southern bank, King Eadred and his cavalry turned their backs on their doomed comrades, their fates sealed by King Eirik's forces.

CHAPTER: EXPELLED

Jórvik, 949

'My lord,' began Oswulf of Bebbanburgh, his voice heavy with a sense of urgency. 'We have received an ultimatum from King Eadred.'

In the grand hall of Jórvik, King Eirik had summoned the ealdormen of Northumbria to discuss the ongoing conflict with King Eadred.

Arinbjørn surveyed the room, acknowledging the nodding heads of the ealdormen before he turned his attention back to Eirik.

'And you, Wulfstan?' inquired Eirik, addressing the archbishop.

Wulfstan shook his head. 'No, my lord. I'm afraid my relationship with Eadred is irreparable. I cannot entertain the notion of reconciliation.'

Eirik nodded gravely. 'Tell me, what does Eadred demand?'

Oswulf stepped forward. 'King Eadred intends to dismantle Northumbria piece by piece until you, Eric Haraldsson, are expelled and the ealdormen pledge allegiance to Wessex.'

Eirik's brows furrowed, his gaze fixed on Oswulf. 'And who does Eadred propose to take my place?'

'Olaf Sithricson,' Oswulf responded, unable to meet Eirik's gaze.

A wry smile played upon Eirik's lips. 'You've tried that

before. What makes you believe it will be different this time?'

'Eadred has launched a series of brutal attacks on our southern border. Villages have been ravaged, lives lost, homes and churches reduced to ashes. Our people suffer, especially as winter sets in,' Oswulf explained, his voice laced with anguish.

Eirik's response was firm, unwavering. 'That is the price of war.'

'But our people are no longer willing to pay that price, my lord,' Oswulf pleaded, the weight of responsibility etched across his features.

'If that is the case, then we must take the fight to Eadred,' proclaimed Eirik.

Oswulf's eyes widened in disbelief. 'How? We would be facing the combined armies of Wessex and Mercia, defenders fighting tooth and nail to protect their homes. Meanwhile, our lands are vulnerable to the raids of Malcolm of Scotland and Olaf of Dublin.'

Eirik fell into a pensive silence. After a thoughtful pause, he finally asked. 'What course of action do you propose, Oswulf?'

The ealdorman met Eirik's gaze, his voice tinged with resignation. 'I fear we have no other choice but to accept Eadred's ultimatum, to spare our people from further suffering.'

Eirik's eyes searched the faces of those present, from Oswulf to Wulfstan, seeking affirmation. The archbishop appeared pale and despondent, yet his unwavering gaze met Eirik's, confirming their shared understanding.

'And is this the collective will of the ealdormen of Northumbria?' Eirik asked, his tone solemn.

One by one, the ealdormen affirmed their support for Oswulf's stance.

Without uttering a single word, Eirik rose from his seat and strode out of the great hall of Jórvik.

CHAPTER: OSWULF

Bebbanburgh, Northumbria, 952

The darkening skies released their chilled rain as Eirik's longship found its resting place on the shore beneath the formidable fortress of Bebbanburgh in the far north of Northumbria. The gusting autumn wind and relentless rain had accompanied them on their journey from the Orkney Islands to these lands.

Eirik and Arinbjørn disembarked, their sea legs unsteady as they stepped on to the sandy ground. Soon, the gates of Bebbanburgh swung open, and a detachment of eight men emerged, marching purposefully towards them.

'King Eric,' one of them announced. 'Lord Oswulf eagerly awaits your arrival. Please follow us.'

Arinbjørn leaned in, his voice barely a whisper. 'You're a king once again?'

Eirik cast a knowing glance at Arinbjørn. 'Come, Gamle,' he beckoned, waiting for his firstborn son to join them.

Silence cloaked their journey to the castle, broken only by the sound of raindrops pelting the ground. Arinbjørn observed the formidable palisade, with its towers and platforms for archers and crossbowmen. Bebbanburgh had endured countless failed attempts at capture by Picts, Scots, Norwegians and Danes, bearing witness to the tumultuous history of this land.

The warmth of the blazing hearth in Oswulf's audience chamber embraced them as they entered, the tantalising scents of food and drink stirring their appetites. However, they refrained from indulging until their host arrived.

'Welcome, King Eric,' a voice resonated behind them. Arinbjørn turned to find Oswulf entering through a side door, his presence commanding the room.

Eirik offered a gracious nod. 'Thank you for extending your invitation, Ealdorman Oswulf. It was an unexpected gesture, three winters after you had me ousted from Jórvik.'

Oswulf met Eirik's gaze. 'I hope it was a welcome surprise.'

'Time will reveal its true nature,' Eirik responded, his voice laden with caution.

'Please, be seated and partake in the feast,' Oswulf invited, waiting for his guests to take their places. 'I am aware of your reservations given our past encounters, and I appreciate the trust you have placed in me by accepting my invitation despite our differences.'

Eirik's eyes surveyed the spread of food before him. 'I have come here to listen. I have yet to make any decisions beyond that.'

'A fair approach,' Oswulf acknowledged, understanding the weight of the choices that lay ahead.

Silence hung in the air for a time as Eirik savoured the food before him, his mind contemplative. Eventually, he spoke, his tone measured. 'Why am I having this conversation with you and not Wulfstan?'

Oswulf's expression darkened. 'Eadred had him arrested. He has languished in prison for years.'

Eirik's voice resonated with sympathy. 'I am sorry to hear of his fate. Wulfstan showed courage in defying the king.'

'He did indeed, and he paid dearly for it,' Oswulf confirmed.

Eirik nodded. 'Tell me, what has changed since you expelled me three winters ago?'

'Some things are different, while others remain the same,'

Oswulf began. 'Olaf Sithricson still cares little for Northumbria, exploiting its resources for his own gains and ferrying them back to Dublin.'

'As you expected he would,' Eirik interjected.

Oswulf continued, undeterred. 'Eadred, on the other hand …'

Eirik listened intently, his curiosity piqued.

'Eadred is plagued by an ailment that slowly saps his strength and vitality. He is absent from council meetings, and others govern in his name. His days are numbered, and he lacks the vigour to mount further incursions into Northumbria.'

Eirik took some time to absorb the information. 'And who stands next in line to the throne?'

'One of Edmund's sons, most likely,' Oswulf surmised.

Eirik's brow furrowed, scepticism evident in his gaze. 'I fail to see why you would extend this invitation to me, or how I would benefit from accepting it.'

Oswulf sighed, weariness etched across his features. 'There are thousands of Danes in Northumbria, inclined to support any Viking warlord over a Saxon ealdorman. If we were to mobilise against Olaf, his forces would be bolstered by Danes fighting for their way of life and their ancient gods.'

Eirik reached for another piece of bread, contemplating Oswulf's words. 'And why would I undertake such a task?'

'Because the heirs of King Harald Fairhair are not fated to a life of pillaging. Your brother sits upon the throne in Norway while you engage in petty raids and sell your slaves in Seville. Your life should be one of honour and renown.'

Eirik's expression hardened, his gaze steady. 'And when Eadred perishes, and the next descendant of Alfred commands me to leave?'

'Then you will leave'—Oswulf's voice trailed off momentarily—'with the spoils, the taxes, and the loyal warriors you have gathered during your time here. With them, you could reclaim the throne of Norway.'

Eirik drained the last of his ale in one swift motion before rising from his seat. He grasped Oswulf's arm firmly, their eyes meeting in an unspoken agreement.

'I accept your offer.'

CHAPTER: JÓL

Jórvik, Northumbria, 952

'This is nice,' Gunnhild remarked, taking in the joyful scene.

Almost the entire family was gathered for the Jól feast in the great hall in Jórvik. Gamle, Guttorm, Harald and Ragnfrød were there, and even Erling, Gudrød and Sigurd had sailed from Denmark to join them. The blazing fire kept them warm and comfortable, and the thin layer of snow covering the ground and the rooftops made her think of Norway.

'And yet, it stirs a longing for home within me,' she continued. 'What news do you have from Norway?'

Arinbjørn, ever the bearer of tidings, shared his insights. 'Haakon is well regarded, but his endeavours to convert the people to the White Christ have faced resistance, particularly in Trøndelag. In Viken, some chieftains remain loyal to Harald Bluetooth.'

'Gunnhild raised an eyebrow. 'And are they loyal to the White Christ as well?'

Arinbjørn nodded. 'Indeed, Harald Bluetooth himself has embraced baptism, and many of his people have followed suit, embracing Christianity.'

'And what of you, Erling?' Gunnhild asked, with a hint of a smirk.

Erling's cheeks reddened, and he cast his eyes downward, his voice slightly hesitant. 'I, too, have been baptised, as have my younger brothers.'

Gunnhild could not help but chuckle. 'King Fairhair granted your father ships and sent him forth to be raised as a Viking. In contrast, we sent you to court, where you were raised as monks. Tell me, what does Harald Bluetooth say about our eventual return to Norway?'

Erling drew this breath and met her gaze. 'He assured me that when the time is right, he will have hundreds of men and two dozen ships ready to support our cause.'

A gleam of satisfaction danced in Gunnhild's eyes. 'Excellent!' She then turned to Eirik, her expression shifting to a more serious tone. 'And what of Olaf Sithricson?'

Eirik let out a weary sigh, his gaze distant. 'Olaf, true to his nature, swiftly retreated to Dublin the moment he caught sight of our ships. He enjoys considerable support there, and they have crowned him king once more. No doubt, he will return to vex us sooner or later.'

Gunnhild's resolve hardened, her eyes filled with determination. 'And when that day comes, you will face him on the battlefield. But for now, let us put aside such worries and revel in this moment of celebration. Let the feast begin!'

CHAPTER: PARLEY

Stainmoor, Northumbria, 954

Tension hung heavy in the air as the warriors prepared for the imminent battle. Gamle voiced his concern. 'Where is Oswulf?'

'He is not here,' King Eirik replied with a touch of disappointment in his voice.

Arinbjørn glanced towards the approaching silhouettes in the south and east and remarked, 'Olaf Sithricson has indeed arrived, as he claimed. He was not wrong about that.'

Eirik's voice held a note of regret. 'Yes, my trust in Oswulf was misplaced, just as his choice of this moor as our battleground.'

Guttorm's voice was tinged with uncertainty. 'Can we flee?'

Arinbjørn considered the question before responding, 'We can, but the difficult terrain and the distance to Jórvik would work against us. Olaf would pursue us relentlessly, picking us off one by one.'

Gamle cast a glance at the enemy ranks. 'They outnumber us.'

Acknowledging the reality, Eirik replied, 'Indeed, they do. Arinbjørn, gather Harald, Ragnfrød and the Einarssons—I need time to think.'

Arinbjørn swiftly carried out the command, and soon the eight men convened to strategize for the upcoming battle.

'Torfinn,' said King Eirik, 'you will take command of the right flank, with two-fifths of our army. Arnkel, you will lead the left flank. Arinbjørn, Gamle, Guttorm, Harald and Ragnfrød, you will remain with me in the centre.'

Arinbjørn could not hide his concern as he spoke. 'That will leave our centre critically weak.'

Eirik's response was unwavering. 'Yes, that is precisely my intention. With our finest hirdmen surrounding us, we will appear weaker than we truly are.'

Arinbjørn held his tongue, understanding the purpose behind Eirik's decision.

'Arinbjørn, Gamle, come with me,' Eirik declared, mounting his horse. 'The rest of you, ensure our forces are prepared and in formation. Now!'

The three rode towards the front lines, stopping midway between the two armies. They waited in silence, and after a while, a delegation of four individuals approached them, one of them holding Olaf Sithricson's banner high.

'A parley?' Olaf smirked. 'Bloodaxe is not known for negotiations.'

Eirik cut him off. 'Why are you here?'

Olaf chuckled, joined by his three henchmen. 'On Lord Oswulf's invitation, no less.'

Eirik's curiosity was piqued. 'That makes two of us. But where is Oswulf?'

Olaf laughed. 'Oh, do not concern yourself with Oswulf. He is safe at Bebbanburgh.'

Eirik pressed further. 'Why? And how do you know this?'

'Because I have had several conversations with Oswulf recently. However, he was quite stubborn until ...' Olaf's voice trailed off.

Eirik prodded, 'Until what?'

'Until Eadred offered him the title of High Reeve of

Northumbria,' Olaf revealed.

Eirik kept his composure. 'And what does that entail?'

'It is the king's highest-ranking representative as Northumbria becomes part of England once more,' Olaf explained.

Eirik's gaze narrowed. 'And what is in it for you?'

'I am the new ealdorman of Jórvik,' Olaf declared. 'Or what remains of Jórvik after Eadred's soldiers are finished with it. They are currently marching towards the city.'

Eirik nodded in understanding. 'Which means King Olaf Sithricson of Dublin becomes the underling to the underling of a sickly Saxon king.'

Olaf shrugged. 'It grants me the right to collect taxes until they expel me once again. I intend to spend most of my time in Dublin.'

Eirik's mind worked quickly. 'If you allow me to leave with my army and exact revenge on Oswulf, you can enter Jórvik without resistance. I have no attachment to these lands.'

Olaf regarded him sceptically. 'A desperate proposal from a desperate man.'

Eirik countered, 'A most profitable proposal for you, nonetheless.'

Olaf shook his head firmly, a hint of stubbornness in his eyes. 'I will not make a truce or treaty with foes, as wise men say. Bloodaxe has thwarted me far too many times already, and I will not let him slip away when he is within my grasp.'

Eirik's resolve hardened, his tone definitive. 'So be it. A battle it shall be.'

With those words, Olaf turned his horse, heading back towards his waiting army. Eirik, Arinbjørn and Gamle followed suit, riding back to their own forces.

'Treason,' Arinbjørn remarked as they regrouped with their army.

'We already knew that,' Eirik responded. 'Saxons make fickle allies.'

Arinbjørn could not help but voice his concern. 'And now, we stand without any allies at all.'

Eirik remained remarkably calm amid the dire situation. Rising in his stirrups, he called out, 'Torfinn and Arnkel Einarsson, join us!'

Soon, Eirik and his four sons, along with Arinbjørn and the two sons of Jarl Torv-Einar of Orkney, were gathered together behind the army.

'What is Olaf doing?' Eirik inquired, his eyes fixed on the enemy lines.

Harald shielded his eyes, observing the movements. 'They are regrouping.'

'How?' Eirik pressed for details.

'They are reinforcing their centre,' Harald replied.

A glimmer of satisfaction crossed Eirik's face. 'Just as I had hoped.'

Arinbjørn could not contain his worry. 'They will charge straight at you, Eirik.'

'Yes, I will be the bait.' Eirik's voice remained resolute. 'Arinbjørn, I have an important task for you.'

Arinbjørn listened intently, somewhat emboldened by Eirik's unwavering composure. 'What is your command, my king?'

'If I should fall, or if it becomes clear that we are on the verge of losing this battle, I need you to take my sons and ride to Jórvik as swiftly as you can. Seek out my wife and any loyal supporters, and sail for the Orkney Islands without delay. Do not linger, for Eadred's soldiers may arrive before you.'

'My king,' Arinbjørn protested, 'my life is not as important. I can hold Olaf's army at bay long enough for you to escape with your sons.'

Eirik's voice carried authority. 'Thank you, Arinbjørn, but that plan will not work. I cannot expect my men to fight without their king, and Olaf will relentlessly pursue me if I was to leave the battlefield.'

Harald stepped forward to support his father's decision. 'Let me stand by your side, Father,' he implored.

Eirik's gaze softened as he looked at his son, filled with paternal love and pride. 'No, Harald. I am an old man, and you and your brothers are the heirs to the throne of Norway. It is not your destiny to end your lives on a desolate moor in a foreign land. Now, obey my commands, all of you. I am still your king.'

CHAPTER: STAINMOOR

'Shields up! Brace yourselves!' King Eirik's voice thundered across the battlefield.

As anticipated, Olaf Sithricson's forces charged through the centre in a wedgelike formation reminiscent of the ancient *svinefylking*. The treacherous terrain slowed their advance, but their sheer numbers threatened to overwhelm Eirik's shield wall.

Arinbjørn, King Eirik, and his sons stood in the fourth rank, with no one behind them. When the Danes collided with the front ranks, Eirik's men were forced to step back, momentarily losing their balance.

'Steady! Two steps at a time!' Eirik's commanding voice cut through the chaos of war. 'Now!'

The thin line of defenders bent under the pressure as the Danes pushed harder against the centre. From the rear, Arinbjørn, Gamle, Guttorm and Harald exerted all their strength, striving to prevent their ranks from breaking.

'The signal! Now!' Eirik called out.

Moments later, Ragnfrød blew a single resounding note with his horn.

Nothing appeared to happen at first, at least not from Arinbjørn's vantage point. He stabbed his sword over the shoulders of the kingsmen in front of him, managing to take the eye of a Dane. To his right, Harald Eiriksson cursed as he fought his way through the chaos, eager to confront the enemy.

But before long, screams emanating from the Danish lines revealed that something had transpired.

'It's working!' Ragnfrød's voice rang out amid the cacophony. 'Torfinn and Arnkel are attacking from both sides. The Danes are trapped!'

The pressure on the centre gradually eased, allowing Eirik and Arinbjørn to step back and assess the situation.

As Ragnfrød had proclaimed, the Danes, pushing recklessly against the weak centre, had unwittingly exposed themselves to a pincer attack as Torfinn and Arnkel struck from the flanks. The enemy found themselves ensnared, unable to manoeuvre or capitalise on their numerical advantage.

Eirik's warriors erupted in cheers as they seized the initiative, striking down the disoriented Danes. Victory seemed within reach.

'They are too many!' a voice cried out amid the chaos.

Arinbjørn and Eirik disengaged from the battle once again.

'They have reinforcements,' Eirik observed.

As they surveyed the field, they saw fresh waves of rested warriors attacking Eirik's flanks, effectively trapping Torfinn and Arnkel's forces between two fronts.

'Saxons,' Arinbjørn added grimly.

'Yes,' Eirik acknowledged.

'Come, let us reinforce the right flank,' Arinbjørn suggested, preparing to move.

'With whom?' Eirik's hand on Arinbjørn's shoulder halted his movement.

Arinbjørn stopped, recognising the truth in Eirik's words.

'No, they are too many,' Eirik declared. 'It is time, Arinbjørn.'

'No, we can still turn the tide!' Arinbjørn's voice trembled with determination. He had never before needed to convince Eirik to continue fighting.

Eirik's gaze held a mix of sadness and resolve. 'I have always known that my life would end on the battlefield. But my legacy does not end with me.'

Eirik removed a massive gold ring from his right arm and fastened it on Arinbjørn's.

'I could never have asked for a better adviser than you, Arinbjørn,' Eirik said, embracing him. 'Nor a more loyal friend. Now, serve my sons as you have served me, until one of them sits on my father's throne.'

Arinbjørn's eyes welled with unshed tears. 'There will be a feast in Valhall tonight, as Odin welcomes the greatest warrior of all to his table.'

Eirik smiled, his face a mix of gratitude and acceptance. 'I will wait for you there, Arinbjørn. Now, go!'

With that, Eirik returned to the battle and pulled his four sons out from the ranks, one by one. He hugged them before lifting his axe and charging into the fray.

'To Valhall!'

With King Eirik's battle cry ringing in his ears, Arinbjørn forced himself to follow his last command. 'Come!' he said to the Eirikssons. 'Find two strong horses each. We must ride many leagues, and time is not on our side.'

Moments later, they rode away from the battleground, first veering northeast to avoid enemy forces before turning southeast towards Jórvik.

From a windswept hilltop east of the battlefield, Arinbjørn and the four Eirikssons stood in grim silence, their gazes locked on the harrowing scene unfurling below. The Danes and Saxons surged forward with relentless determination, their victory seemingly assured. The once mighty shield wall of

Eirik's forces crumbled under the unyielding onslaught.

Arinbjørn's heart plummeted, a heavy weight settling upon his chest. The loss of hope was palpable as Eirik's banner, the last symbol of their resistance, fell to the ground. A surge of sorrow mingled with anger coursing through his veins.

Unable to find the words to express his despair, Arinbjørn turned his steed and slowly descended the eastern slope of the hill, the chilling wind biting at his face. The bitter taste of defeat lingered in his mouth, but he refused to succumb entirely to desolation.

Harald galloped alongside Arinbjørn, his voice cutting through the silence. 'Where are we going, Arinbjørn?'

'We must reach Jórvik before Eadred's soldiers,' Arinbjørn replied, his voice tinged with resolve.

'And then?' Harald pressed.

'Home,' Arinbjørn declared, the word carrying a spark of hope. 'To claim your rightful title as the king of Norway.'

Arinbjørn's heart surged with a renewed sense of purpose as their horses thundered ahead, embarking on their race against time.

VIKINGS OF NORWAY

Meet the Vikings of Norway, the Norse Kings and the legendary figures from the sagas!

The chronological order of the series is as follows:

The Viking Ventures
Harald Fairhair
Bloodaxe
Haakon the Good

However, every book is a standalone story and they can be read in any order.

Viking Ventures

Fairhair

Eric Bloodaxe

Haakon The Good

Printed in Great Britain
by Amazon

41741861R00139